# *Dear Rafe*

## Rolando Hinojosa

Arte Público Press
Houston, Texas
1985

Arte Publico Press
University of Houston
Houston, TX  77204-2090

Second Printing, 1991
Copyright©1985 by Rolando Hinojosa
LC 84-072299
ISBN 0-934770-38-7

The paper used in this publication meets the requirements
of the American National Standard for Permanence of
Paper for Printed Library Materials Z39.48-1984. ∞

Printed in the United States of America

## First Dedication

This work (that Puritan word) is dedicated to two veterans of World War II; to two scholars; and, to two men worthy of love and respect.

Two plus two plus two equals six, and since this number is divisible by three, I speak of two friends, Luis Leal and Américo Paredes, whom RH loves, appreciates, and admires.

We Spanish Basques invented a compass
which pointed directly to the human soul,
but it was either stolen or broken, or
both. It wants re-inventing.

> Fermín Zuloaga, SJ
> 1776-1845

# Dear Rafe

## Part I.

Jehu Malacara's Letters to Rafe Buenrostro
Chapters:   1-23

## Part II.

P. Galindo's Soundings and Findings
Chapter:   24   Polín Tapia
Chapter:   25   Ira Escobar
Chapter:   26   Martin San Esteban
Chapter:   27   Viola Barragán
Chapter:   28   Bowly T.G. Ponder
Chapter:   29   Olivia San Esteban
Chapter:   30   Viola Barragán
Chapter:   31   Rebecca Escobar
Chapter:   32   Sammie Jo Perkins
Chapter:   33   Arnold Perkins
Chapter:   34   E.B. Cooke
Chapter:   35   Rufino Fischer Gutiérrez
Chapter:   36   Bowly T.G. Ponder
Chapter:   37   Mrs. Ben (Edith) Timmens
Chapter:   38   P. Galindo, the wri
Chapter:   39   Eugenio & Isidro Peralta: Klail City Twins
Chapter:   40   Lucas Barrón
Chapter:   41   Polín Tapia
Chapter:   42   Vicente de la Cerda
Chapter:   43   Emilio Tamez
Chapter:   44   Arturo Leyva, B.B.A.
Chapter:   45   Esther Lucille Bewley
Chapter:   46   Don Javier Leguizamón
Chapter:   47   Jovita de Anda Tamez

## Part III.

Conclusions:   1. A Penultimate Note
               2. Brass Tacks Are Better: They Last Longer

# A Reasonable Explanation of Things to Come*

What follows in Parts I and II consists of some firsthand facts and of diverse opinions, not all of which are soundly based or well-verified; there are also some asides and some commentary as well as other assorted data, dates, and events which (on the one hand) are well-known or which (on the other hand) are not and thus must be deduced.

The writer (The wri) is convinced that not all bases are sufficiently covered in Part I, and so in Part II, he intends to add a shading of his own once in a while, but always on the side of truth, that necessary element.

Warning: The wri is not out to prove something beforehand and thus he expects to earn his reliability, his trustworthiness. The wri (considering his state of health) is also in no position to play fast and loose with the facts; he promises, furthermore, to go to the heart and core of the matter. He can hardly do anything else being, as he is, at game's end. He's been dealt the last card, and, alas, it's a singleton.

Background. The wri, interned as he was at the Wm. Barrett Veterans' Hospital, received a packet of letters addressed to and read originally by Rafe Buenrostro (Atty. at Law and currently a lieutenant of detectives in the District Attorney's office in Belken County). The letters had been written to him by his cousin, Jehu Malacara, at that time, the chief loan officer at the Klail City First National Bank.

The wri was convalescing at Wm.B. V.A. Hosp. as a result of a liverish condition. The liver (that treacherous organ) is unable to defend itself against the smallest serving of 3.2 beer; both the liver and the wri, then, are in a bad way. Why? Ah, and you may well ask: drink, pure and simple. There is an accompanying shortness of breath: the wri has been a heavy smoker these last twenty years and thus one must add a lung deficiency as a corollary.

---

* Verbum sap.

The icing on the cake came when Barney Craddock, Capt., M.D., came up with a further diagnosis: basal carcinoma. Not much, no, but just enough to spot the face here and there. In short, that's all the wri needed 1) to call it a day, 2) a night, 3) quits.

As for Rafe, who remained a patient there when the wri left, he was making his third tour of duty at the hospital; those scars above his left eye are due to injuries suffered during the Korean fracas and now, almost nine years after the fact, some high explosive fragments are cropping up and around the eyebrows, and, according to the oculists, these may bother his eyesight if not attended to. Nothing major, they say, but they should not be neglected at this time, etc., and one knows how doctors are.

An explanation: The wri doesn't have much time left; some eight months, perhaps nine, which may be enough for someone's gestation unless the kid's a seven-monther; 7-months have been known to appear in the best and in the worst of families. A matter of one's point of view, to be sure.

Time (a new topic) can eat through almost anything: friendships, loyalties, love, hearts, et alii. It marches, ambles, and races on, although at times it lays in wait, too. and, sometimes it merely goes away, like teenage acne. Obviously, time can do anything and the proof's usually in the mirror. Time, then, is something that the wri has little of; those eight months we talked about earlier. The wri acknowledges that this may be his last contribution to the Klail City entries; there's no need to cry or to wear sack cloth, brothers. Time is really nothing more than Hell all dressed up and with no place to go.

The wri has had more pleasant moments on the planet than the law may allow; no complaints, then. He does, however, recognize that he could have used his time in a more profitable manner, but he could be wrong about that, too. (The wri also acknowledges that he has been wrong in times past.)

What follows, and this is gospel, are the latest findings in re Jehu Malacara, the man/child born in Relámpago, Texas, and reared in Klail City, county seat of Belken County.

Final *caveat*: Belken County *mexicanos*, aside from their northern Mexican Spanish language, speak English, by and large; the Belken County Anglo Texans, aside from their predominant Midwestern American English, also speak Spanish, by and large. Proximity creates psychological bonds and proximity also breeds children, as we've been told. The truth, then, *über alles*.

At this writing, Rafe Buenrostro is either on his way home from the V.A. Hospital or about to be released; it was a longer stay than either he or the doctors had reckoned. As for Jehu, there's no telling where he is, and hence this story.

*Sufficit.*

# Part I

# The Letters

# 1

Dear Rafe:

Here's wishing you a hale and hearty and hoping to hear that you're doing better, much better. According to Aaron, he claims you look as thin and pale as a whooping crane, and all I can say is "Fatten up, cousin," and you'll be up and out of that hosp. before you know it.

Not much to tell about the Valley right now, but things'll pick up when the primaries come around. The job at the Bank is a job at the Bank, and you'd be surprised (most prob. not) about how some people run their lives in Klail and in Belken County. Not a matter of a three-alarmer, no, but their accounts reveal that all is not well with some of the citizens in our tip of the L.S. State.

The trial for those killers you uncovered has been set for next Jan. 8. You're sure to be up and around by then; will you then be asked to testify?

Since you'll be in exile in Wm. Barrett for a while, I'll keep you up-to-date, as far as I can, on the doings here. For now, then, the primaries which are just around the corner.

Yesterday, and what follows is rumor, gossip, and hearsay, my boss, Noddy Perkins, called Ira Escobar into his office; it's sound-proof, of course, and late that afternoon, Ira called on the inter-office phone: "Got to see you, Jehu." I initialed the tellers' accounts, popped my head in Noddy's office, and said good-night to him. On my way to the back lot, there's Ira again.

He could hardly stand it, whatever *it* was, and then, in a rush, he said that Noddy "and some very important persons, Jehu" had talked to him seriously and on a high level. It happens that our Fellow Texans want Ira to stand for County Commissioner Place Four. And, what did I think a-that?

My heart didn't miss a beat, needless to s., and poor Ira felt a bit deflated. Neither of us said a word for a second or more until I hit him for a light after having first accepted one of his cigarettes. (Ira's dumb, but not *that* dumb). He saw that, far from envy, it was plain disinterestedness on my part, but he still wasn't sure about my reaction or lack of it.

He looked at me again and asked if I didn't have any earthly I-de-ah what THAT meant : Noddy and the very imp. pers. wanted and had *asked* him to run, and that they were ready (and standing in line, I suppose) to help him all the way.

Wherever that may happen to lead, say I. But, who am I to go around breaking hearts and illusions? By now you're prob. way ahead of me here since the only thing Ira was interested in was to let me know the Good News, and that was it.

Forward! Haaarch! The last thing he'd want from me would be some advice, and I'm not good at that either. There we were, two lonely people in a treeless parking lot, at 6 p.m., with 97 degrees F staring us in the face, and Ira saying: "Jay, Jay, don't you see? County Commissioner Place Four, the *fat* one, Jay." (Yes, he calls me *Jay*). About all I could think of was to wonder what Noddy, the Ranch, the Bank, etc. were up to this time; I mean, they already own most of the land 'in these here parts' and they have ALL THAT MONEY, SON; so it's prob. something else in that woodpile aside from the wood, right? I finally shook his hand, or the other way round, and then he went straight home to give his wife the second surprise of her life.

Ira and his wife are new to Klail, and I'm fairly certain you don't know her; her name's Rebecca Caldwell (we who know and love her, call her *Becky*) and she's from Jonesville-on-the-Rio. Her father's a Caldwell, but a Mexican for a' that. Her mother's a Navarrete, and enough said. I've seen her a couple of times at a Bank party and other Bank doings and what-not.

The phone! A call from one of the relatives in Relámpago; Auntie Enriqueta says she's coming along nicely; nothing serious. (Remember when we used to hit Relámpago fairly often? I wonder whatever-happened-to-those-baldheaded-tattooed-twins, Doro and Thea, right?). Anyway, getting back to Becky, she's a bit of a looker. We get along, and we do look each other in the eye when we've said 'hello' and such. Nice looking face to go with a well-rounded little *bod*. We'll see.

Now, it could be it's a false alarm, and it may be that the Central Powers are merely testing our boy here. You never know. If

Noddy *were* testing the waters, and Ira's enthusiasm showed through, Noddy could read that as our boy's willingness to serve the public.

Old Man Vielma sends his best; ran into him at the Blue Bar. In re his daughter who now shares a house with your former sister-in-law, Delfina, our illuminated friends are up in arms about 'those two shameless women who live together.' Why go on? As you can see with that one good eye you've got left, we're still as nice and as sweet and understanding in Klail City as ever.

Well, cuz, take care, eat well, and I'm sure that before either one of us knows it, you'll be back hard at work at the Court House. (Thought I'd make your day: Sheriff Parkinson, he of the big feet, is taking much of the credit for solving those murders you and Culley and Sam cleared up. Big Foot's no fool; he says it was his *office* that solved them, and since he is the sheriff . . .)

Best,
Jehu

# 2

Dear Rafe:

First off: kindly do excuse the delay in answering your latest; it has to do with the work here, a rush on time, and then, before I know it, two weeks have come and gone, and I haven't dropped you line one. Second excuse: attended and participated in a sad funeral: don Pedro Zamudio's, that old Oblate of Mary Immaculate, who graced the fair city of Flora long and well.

It happens that he had two older brothers (yes, *older*), and they came down from God only knows what aerie of His. Black hats, hooked-noses, and as bald as Father Pedro himself. Half the world and most of Belken County showed up, and I almost broke up thinking on that grand and glorious burial we gave Bruno Cano that bright Spring morning years ago. It's rained here and snowed elsewhere since that time, son. And now, sic transit.

On the way back to Klail, I stopped off at the old mexicano cemetery near Bascom. One of those things, I guess; I walked around reading the stones and markers, looking over the old and loved names. As you know, we're all one day nearer the grave.

*Public Notice*: The offer to Ira appears to be on the level. Noddy Perkins' sister (more on her in a minute) came by the Bank *eins-zwei-drei* times, and where there's smoke, there's a political barbecue, right?

Tidy-up time: you're wrong on the Escobar familial relationships, and I'll explain why in short order. Ira's an Escobar on his father's side (old don Nemesio Escobar, who's related to the Prado families from Barrones, Tamaulipas. Got that?) But, Ira also happens to be a Leguizamón, sad to say, and it comes from the maternal end of things: A Leguizamón-Leyva for a mother who's from Uncle Julian's generation. Of course, if you were to see Ira, you'd pick him out in a crowd, straight off. It's the nose and jaw that gives the Leguizamóns away every time. And, as far as the Bank job's concerned, he got *that* because of his Leguizamón connections (this from Noddy, by the way). That aside, if I were Ira, I'd watch Noddy P. NP's not a lost babe, and our boy Ira is, in a word, blinded by the goal that glitters. To sum up, then, he looks as easy a prey as a jackass flats bunny, wide-eyed (and blind), ears pointed up (and deaf as a door), and ready for someone to pick him off with a .22 long. He seems to love it, though. It's God's truth that there's always someone who's willing to do anything in this world.

Ira himself told me that he'll pay the filing fee at the Court House this p.m. I've no proofs, of course, but I'm dead sure Noddy's got something up that sleeve of his'n. Yes, he do. I've been here three years now, and I've barely scratched three or four layers in that man's make-up. And he goes much deeper'n that, believe me.

As for you, I've got another surprise: you know Noddy's sister. Yes, you do. Ready? No less a body than Mrs. Kirkpatrick, our old Klail H.S. typing inst. Remember this?

A S D F G & don't look at the key
Q W E R T & keep your eyes on me!

Yep! Powerhouse Kirkpatrick is Noddy Perkins' sib. (The first time she saw me at the bank, must be going on three years now, she spotted me in my office & said, "Are you the Buenrostro boy?")

Well! I knew *she* knew who I was (it's their bank, dammit, and they know who they hire) but I went along, & we both wound up laughing and what-all. Getting up in years is Old Powerhouse, and widowed all these twenty years, Jehu, but I've got all my teeth, she says. (And all that money Tinker Kirkpatrick left her, too, sez I). Her main interests these days revolve round the Klail City Woman's Club & the Music Club. If she rules there the way she did at Klail High, God help 'em.

By the by, Ira's not to run for Place Four, as he'd been told. (There's a note of sadness to that 'as he'd been told,' isn't there?)

This is what I think the play will be:

Ira's to run v. Morse Terry (Place Three) in the Democratic Primary. Do you recall MT? He was up at Austin with us; speaks Spanish (natch), and he's a friend of the mexicano. Sure he is. (Same old lyrics to Love's Old Sweet Song).

Here's the story, Your Honor: Looks like some toes were stepped on; or maybe a double cross or two, not sure, but *something* happened. Big, too. Soooo, Noddy's lining up some of our Fellow Texans against Morse Terry, and backing Ira Escobar.

Talk about your strange bedfellows. The rundown: Ira v. Terry with Bank backing, and our fair-haired boy's on his way to the victory circle. I can imagine Ira at night, alone, and softly, in the bathroom, facing the mirror, that Ira sees himself as a future Congressman in Washington; how's *that* for a dream? Still, stranger things have happened, mirabile visu et dictu.

There *is* one problem, however, and thus Powerhouse's comings and goings: Noddy wants Ira's wife's admission to the Woman's Club, and that's a tall order, Chief. More on this later as soon as the news develops.

Next week this here cousin a-yours is off to the Big House for a kickoff Bar-B-Q; Ira's announcement, most prob. One of the girls at the Bank says that a lot of people (she put the stress on *people*) have been invited out there; I'll keep you posted.

And, too, word of honor and, as a relative, I'll say more in re Noddy and his antecedents although this may just be repeating something you already know. Correct me if I'm wrong.

Gotta go. Am enclosing a pix; the girl on the left is a current one.

Best,<br>Jehu

# 3

Dear Rafe:

Well, sir, you take the cake *and* the icing; the words 'excuse me' are still a part of the lexicon, & I'll wait for them. And, furthermore, erase, expunge, and take away all of your *feelthy* thoughts, you cad. Strange as it may seem, to you, I *have* been known to have the very best of honorable intentions, at times. Well, enough said & amen. Keep the picture and apologize to it.

What I'd promised in re Noddy:

Noddy Perkins is a man just short of his mid-sixties; his parents were fruit tramps who showed up in the Valley just before the times of the Seditious Ones; that puts it around 1915 or so. His old man was killed by a freight train & cut up in halves or thirds, depending on who's telling the story. Some of those who say they remember, attest that 1) the old man had been drinking; 2) that he merely stumbled on the tracks on his way home. Noddy's no souse, by the way; a daily highball or two, but that's about it. He likes to be in control, you see.

Echevarría (a long time ago) told me that Noddy didn't have a pot or a down payment for one when he married Blanche Cooke; a head for business, yes, then and now. (He speaks Spanish, oh, yes, & he likes for his mexicano hands to call him *Norberto* when he dresses up like a Laredo cowboy on weekends. I keep telling you: it takes all sorts to populate Belken County. Pay attention).

He hired me (personally) some three years ago; he knew me from Klail Savings, of course (which the Ranch also owns); of course. That piece of information must come as a first-class shock to you. As you may know, we've no branch banking in Texas; not yet, anyway.

His wife, Blanche, aka Miz Noddy, Mrs. Perkins, etc. has been slightly burned by both the sun and Oso Negro gin. She's got a natural enough tan, and her voice is a bit mushy with a touch of hoarseness. The martinis get a goodly share of the blame for that, I suspect. Doesn't show up here much, but when she does or whenever she's back from her 'periodic drying out' as her dearest friends call it, she and Noddy go over to the Camelot Club or maybe to the beach to celebrate her return.

One of the V.P.'s here, he's also the Cashier, is a full-fledged member of the Cooke-Blanchard clan. Of course, of course. His name's E.B. Cooke (he's called Ibby) and he thinks Texas mexicanos were put in the Valley for the family's absolute convenience. We get along, neither well nor badly; we just get. In other words, it's 'good morning' in the a.m., and 'good evening' at closing time. And that, after my first two years here; a word to the unlearned. Noddy hired me, so I work for him is Ibby's thinking; but he's up front about it which is a blessing.

Noddy's wife gets along with Powerhouse; prob. has no option or say so in the matter. At any rate, they share different interests, as Powerhouse says. But make no mistake: they *all* get along & more so when it's family v. anybody else. The spoiled darling here is Sammie Jo; two marriages, as you know, no kids, but this and that you already know. *We* still get along just fine, thank you.

Back to Noddy's father: he was called Old Man Raymond; Raymond was the font name, and the old mexicanos remember him as that. In English, too: Olmén Reymon.

Old Man Raymond died not only mangled but broke as well, and Noddy must've had a hard time of it for a while. (No one talks about Noddy's mother; not a word). Now, how he came to marry someone like Blanche Cooke is a mystery to me; one thing, I don't think he caused the alcohol problem, although one never knows. As you know, Sammie Jo's our age, and so NP must have married kinda late, right?

Noddy has 1) few illusions &, 2) less friends. It could be that he has the type of friend the rich have, BUT! in Klail, who's rich, besides them?

One more thing, he won't rattle. To be sure, he's got more than half the deck in his hand at all times; still, you've got to see him in action. Nota Bene: you've got to watch him every second; don't turn your back on him. He's the type that'll watch your hide dry.

And that's about the book on NP.

Must close, cuz.

Best,
Jehu

# 4

Dear Rafe:

A short note. The sample ballots are out! The primaries will soon be with us, & from there it's the general elections in Nov. The latest gunk: Morse Terry has encountered a certain difficulty raising enough funding for his re-election. And our Ira? Very well, and thankee kindly.

I did promise over the teleph. to tell you something about the Bar-B-Q, and here goes:

They just flat-out invited everybody. A lovely woman (Anglo Texan; an atom or two on the chunky side, and somewhat myopic, I'd say) sat next to me; I was putting up with a long and fairly frayed story being told as only Mrs. Ben Timmens can tell 'em. God-it-was-long. (Chile & Peru went to war, signed a peace treaty, resumed normal relations, were up in arms again, and she still wasn't through). But, get through she did, & the arriviste piped up: "Well, just how many Mexicans *did* Noddy invite?" I was sitting the closest to her, and the others there tried to muzzle her, but she wasn't having any. She went on & on, and there was mortification & embarrassment all around until she spotted Powerhouse, yoohooed to her, & there she went.

Sighs of relief, some coughing (and hemming and hawing), anything; anything to make up, soften, a — mel — io — rate the sit — u — a — tion don't you know.

I think it's healthy to see & hear this type of shit once in a while; it's both sobering & reassuring to know that all's not well with the world.

Oh, before I forget completely, guess who else was there? None other than María Téllez, bright, bushy-tailed, and in living color. She walks & she talks, and there's blocs and piles of votes in that purse of hers.

No secret that she and Noddy mixed business & pleasure up to a few years ago. But, now it's all business, from what I can see. They made a lovely couple

It's a bit sad, though. María's not being counted for too much on Ira's race; she's here, & she's of the company, but not *in*. Oh, she'll help in the other primary races, sure, but not in Ira's; this is something special. Everything is being handled by an advertising outfit from Jonesville. Very professional.

NP's not thinking of taking out a lease on Ira; he wants him lock, stock, and bbl. Is there any doubt? Try this one on: the sample ballots just came out, right?, but Ira's portrait was alrealy nailed to just about every telephone pole & palm tree in Belken County. You can't miss seeing him since they're on both sides of the highway. Running for *one* precinct and money is being spent from Jonesville to Edgerton and from Ruffing to Relámpago. Ho, ho!

According to those mexicanos who should know better, Morse Terry is in trouble because he's a friend to the mexicano. We never do learn, do we? Many of us still hold on for dear life to that 'friend of the mexicano' bull. Those mexicanos who've been bought & paid for and are now resting in Noddy's hip pocket, say that Ira Escobar represents The New Breed. My God! Don't they *know* what they're saying? Yes, I know what you're saying: Obviously not, obviously not.

And would you look at this: according to one of the Bank secretaries, (a Texas Anglo), she says that Sammie Jo herself sponsored Ira's wife for the Woman's Club. (The sec.'s name is Esther Bewley; she's one of the small-ranch Bewleys. Do you happen to remember some po' whites called Posey? They're all related). Anyway, Esther says that the road had already been cleared, graded, & paved when SJ nominated Becky Escobar.

A lot of pressure, and many of Klail's first & finest fumed & cussed & spit & swore & what-all, but in the end, economic reason prevailed. Noddy has outstanding notes on *everybody*, & all it takes is a little jiggle of the rope, & that's it. There are hints, and then there are *hints* spelled with a capital $. After Sammie Jo's nominating speech (she now wears contacts, by the way), Powerhouse seconded it with a longish speech of her own, and, as a capper, Bonnie Shotwell (gotcha!) spoke in favor of Becky Escobar. Not a black ball in the lot, & now Mrs. Escobar is in the Woman's Club.

Today the Woman's Club, tomorrow the Music Club. Hut-toop-hip-fo-ah. . .

Hey! What can I tell you about Ira Escobar?

Had enough?

Best,
Jehu

# 5

Dear Rafe:

Lunch at the Camelot; Noddy sent me, & *sent's* the proper word, son. It's a new piece of business: Noddy would like to shed the car agency, & the prospective buyer is to use the bank's money for said purpose. (We sell, he borrows from us. Can't lose).

Took two hours, & I really didn't have to since I'll sic the lawyers in for most of the paper work anyway. Still two hours away from the Bank are two hours away from the Bank, & what one learns at the Camelot, isn't learned anywhere else.

From what I hear, some recalcitrants are still somewhat unhappy about Becky Escobar's membership. All I can say to that is, T.S., girls, it's *their* town, not yours. Truth may be beauty and beauty truth, but in Klail, truth is hell absolute.

I'm telling you: the Music Club is the next target of opportunity; Noddy can do whatever he damn well pleases and whenever he well damn pleases, and what are you gonna do about it, Slick?

Sammie Jo passed by when the client and I were picking at our food, and it seemed as if everyone there stopped eating. Did I say *seemed*? I'd swear on it. She stopped, I lit her cigarette, & she walked away. She really doesn't give a damn, you know. Oh, but she's a lick, and half of the women there now brush *their* hair the way *she* does.

Care to make a bet? The day *she* stops smoking. THEY'LL STOP. I mean, she won't even have to *give* the order. ¡Viva Klail City! But:

Back to business. The client's a car dealer in Wm. Barrett & Houston; deals with his local banks, as he should, but for *this* transact., he borrows from us or it's *adiós*. Oh, he's got the money, all right, (we've checked), and, as always, the life insurance we require, for slightly more than the loan itself, in this case $700,000. He'll buy from Blanchard-Cooke Underwriters. That's no broom, son, that's an upright Hoover sucking that gold dust. He also pays the premiums for us, the beneficiaries, in case of untimely demise. The higher cost of the cars is passed on to the consumer, of c.

I'll tell you this, though, with all this talk about money, we seldom see it: one talks about resources, figures, sums, etc, but we don't soil our Christian hands with it. I was *born* to be a banker; predestined, you see.

Change of subj. Do you (happen to) remember Elsinore Chapman? (God! What a perfectly *stupid* question!) Anyway, about the time you went up to the hosp., she was back in Klail; childless & husbandless, yeah. And then she was in a wreck just east of Ruffing, and it was fairly serious. She'd been in the hosp. there for some twenty days or so and doing well, when all of a sudden, she died; just like that. (Either Pennick or Morley told me about it; I can't recall which one). I felt slightly ill; I couldn't explain it to anyone then or now, and I imagine that may be a natural enough feeling. I didn't care for her that much, but I was saddened by the news, all the same.

As per your request, I did go see Acosta about your farm land; he'll be out of town for a while, but I left word for him to call me at the Bank. Israel and Aaron have been alerted.

Best,
Jehu

# 6

Dear Rafe:

Glad to hear you're doing much better up there; Israel and Aaron were here yesterday, (Sun.), and we had us some beer, some meat, and much talk, & most of that was politics. You know how *that* goes. Israel's little Rafe is a Buenrostro through & through; he doesn't call me 'uncle,' it's 'Jehu this' or 'Jehu that.' And you ought to see him walk around: hands in pockets, eyes on the ground, and taking long strides. Even-tempered little guy, and he doesn't seem to give Israel or your sister-in law much trouble.

They said that on the way to town, they saw some new billboards on several country roads: IRA ESCOBAR BELIEVES IN BELKEN COUNTY. Now what the hell does *that* mean? Nothing, right? But that's what it's all about. The signs are in red, white, and blue. (I've three ball points and a slew of gofer matchbooks and some desk blotters. For ball points?)

Noddy (and the Leguizamóns, say I) are spending m u c h o d i n e r o. Ira's out and off for most of the day, and things are looking bad for Morse Terry.

Last night: another barbecue. This one was held at Raymond Perkins Field; Noddy's cowboys cooked the meat; some of them played the music, and of course we-all had us a dance. Us, by the way, means the mexicanos in this case.

I took a date along: Olivia San Esteban (Hi, there!). I'm not letting any more grass grow around these feet, no sir. Do you remember Ollie? She returned to Austin after giving it the college try at teaching high school. She's now a pharmacist in partnership with her brother, Martin. Him you remember, and he's still a pain.

Finally met Ira's wife as a political person. Butter wouldn't melt there, kid. Right off, *she* told Ollie she'd been to school at North Texas State; a music major. And then she talked about the Woman's Club, and, are you ready? She then asked Ollie, 'Do you belong, Olivia? I mean, are you affiliated?'

And Ira? Smiling like a cat eating grits. Ollie then said that her mother didn't let her go out in the daytime much. Becky didn't react at all; a-tall, as she says it. Well, from there she talked of Denton, Texas, as if it were the world's own belly button which, to my way of reckoning, must be some 180 degrees off, but no matter: she's really more of a Leguizamón than they are; and that is saying a lot, ain't it?

And you guessed it, she doesn't dance *those* dances nor 'at those dances' either. Don't come telling me that Noddy didn't know what he was doing. (But with all that, she's not mean spirited; and, she's got a great body. We get along jes' fine.)

This morning, at the bank, Ira told me that Becky enjoyed our talk and that she 'had a ball, a real ball,' and that she'll see to it that Ollie becomes a member of the Woman's Club. At times, at work, I really need a drink now and then.

After the Bar-B-Q, Ollie and I went for some coffee and coco-nut-pie at the Klail City Diner where we met up with Noddy, his sister-in-law, Anna Faye, and A.F.'s husband, Junior Klail. We talked about everything, but it was mostly politics; we wound up closing the place around one o'clock.

Morse Terry's name did crop up a couple of times, and despite the beating he's getting in the barbecues and on the airwaves, no one said a mean word against him. Not one. My head was spinning trying to figure out just what *that* meant, but I gave up; you go figure it.

Junior Klail, in the flesh there, sits atop some $37 million by hisself alone; this according to Noddy, and *he* should know. Let me tell you a recent story: When some national TV station said something on an editorial commentary, and Junior Klail didn't like it, he (supposedly, now) fired off some telegrams to Paley at CBS or to somebody in NBC. According to those 'in the know' there was some sort of apology from them. As you may recall, Junior's name is Rufus T., just like our Founding Father, and Junior must be the 3rd or 4th one of the line. Although he's nudging sixty, he's still called Junior, and I imagine it's better than calling him Rufus III or Rufus IV, both of which sound a bit like a king or a racehorse or something.

Take care, and what option have you to do otherwise?

Best,
Jehu

# 7

Dear Rafe:

The Democratic (and only) primaries have come & gone, and the winner!!!!, Ira Escobar! Everybody adores a good loser, so Morse Terry announced he'd now run as an *independent*. An independent? In Belken? At any rate, there are three months between now and the Nov. elecs., and neither side is talking prisoners.

The change in IE is unbelievable; people can say what they want to, but seeing is *not* believing. There's radiance in that face, his eyes glaze, and then they kindle and shine. Also, he is most obliging (to his lessers), don't you know. The only thing needed now is for him to call Noddy by his first name; and this he'll try in time. (As for Noddy, he contributes to both sides of the Demo. factions; as he says: 'They're both ours.' I like that, and it further confirms what I've said about the old pirate, whatever else he may be, he's no hypocrite. Ira'd better watch himself, that's all.)

Esther Bewley tells me that Becky's a true convert to the cause: there's no more faithful adherent to the rules and regs. of the Woman's Club than B. And I like that, too, I want you to know; no half measures there, son. He who is not with me, right?

Just the other day, according to Esther, Becky spoke on patriotism, loyalty, and maternal love. Applause, and then a standing ov., followed by a joining of hands and a singing of *Texas Our Texas*, the *Star Spangled Banner* (first verse only, please) and then *The Eyes of Texas*. The *Eyes*? Oh, well.

Work here at the B., is going on as it always does: a signature there, and then Ollie and I see each other on weekends (and at other times whenever the weather and the curse permit).

I finally got Acosta as per your inst. and took him over to the Court House. Everything's in order there: taxes all paid up, the property lines well-marked and defined, and no changes whatsoever. Of course, he'll still have the Leguizamóns as his next door neighbors, as did our grandfathers and before. I then called Israel and Aaron on this and mailed copies of the deeds, etc. by special deliv.

Now, the one who appeared at the B. this morning was Noddy's wife; she came out of nowhere, before the doors were open. She looked a bit on the trembly-wembly side and stiff-jointed. Her hair was a touch bluer than usual, and in spite of the heat, she wore long, formal gloves and had her head covered by a see-through scarf covering her sparse hair.

I told Esther to open the door, take her by the arm, and to make her comfortable; I quick-timed it to Noddy's office and himself dashed out, and we both brought her to his office. (Time for her visit to the spa, poor thing.) Her driver was at the backdoor *in less than fifteen minutes* — all the way from the Ranch, too. He's supposed to take care of her, and *how* she got to the Bank, no one knows. I went with her and the driver to the Ranch, & she didn't say a word to me, but it was nothing personal. She wasn't focusing too well, and she may have been thinking about her trip to Colorado where she'll stay until the next time.

Sammie Jo was at pool side as usual, and right before either of us said much, Powerhouse K., came out of nowhere and said, 'Got something to tell you, Jehu.' SJ winked, pointed at me, and dove in again.

It wasn't anything: she wanted to pass on some Valley history to me; she spoke about the time Pancho Villa came to the Valley, to Ruffing, acc. to her, and how Villa tore up tracks, held up a train, etc. She said she'd seen the dead and the burned and then that Villa etc. etc. You and I both know she's talking about the Seditionists of '15. The closest Villa came to Valley must have been 800 mi., but there she was with her 70 years in the Valley and Villa did this, and that, and the other. Why argue, right? During all of this, of course, Sammie Jo was in and out of the pool. Powerhouse finally went into the house, came out again, and drove to town. SJ walked over, smiled that smile, and I stayed for coffee.

From there to the bank, driven back, my boy, and just in the nick to see don Javier Leguizamón himself. What could I possibly tell you? Himself looked well and lost no time in reminding Noddy that I worked for him when I was a kid. Prob. takes credit for my job here, too, for all I know. You think he mentioned Gela Maldonado to Noddy? You take that bet, & you lose.

I swear that this may just be the very first time I've heard Himself speak English; better than avge., too.

I gave Noddy the high sign about things at home, and he understood; as I walked by, he reached out and put his hand on my shoulder. (Does care about her, doesn't he?)

Ira is beside himself (to coin a phr.) and he can taste that oh-so-sweet (and heady) wine of victory. The other day, right after work, I told him to relax, settle down. After all, we're talking about *one* precinct in *one* county out of 254 in this grand and oily state of ahs. Well, shit, he looked at me as if I had called his mother a dirty name. I'm telling you, Ira believes he may just wind up in Washington in two-three years; some hope!

The one who's even more carried away by all of this is Becky. We had some coffee this aft. in my office. Gotcha! One does need to be careful, though. She's got pretty brown eyes. Nice mouth, too. But it was business, and I kept my mind mostly on that.

Ira's convinced that he invented moveable type. And, *now*, he bends my tone-deaf ear on interest rates, points, and, *and*, the National Debt, for Christ's sake! (Sammie Jo's thrilled at the pilgrim's progress. Told me so herself.)

It's been a busy day, but here's a mild surprise for you: don Javier Leguizamón Himself asked me about you. Ha! He wondered, he says, how our lieutenant of detectives was getting along. *Our*, he said. I told him you were well and enjoying life up at the V.A. Hosp. No reaction. And so it goes in Klail City, son.

Best,<br>Jehu

NB See here, you can hardly lay the blame at my innocent feet: I sent the ball points fully expecting them to work. Now then, it turns out that they don't. Look at it this way: maybe there's something symbolic there. By the way, mine doesn't work either.

# 8

Dear Rafe:

Guess what? Ira, our Ira, doesn't drink; not at all. Not even a beer; allergies, he says. Now, whoever heard of a Valley boy who didn't drink beer? Damndest thing you've ever seen.

Last Sun., our cousin Santana Campoy came through with a smallish barbecue; political, what else. But just for the guys. There were also some twenty upriver Anglo Texans there.

Talk was about this & that, and old political stories, and there was Ira holding on to an RC Cola with one hand and a beefed-up tortilla on the other. He then told a joke (first in Spn. and then in Eng.) and there was polite laughter here and there. The company was a bit fast for IE, and this leads me to ask: where was he raised? Doesn't he have a sense of humor? He really isn't a bad guy, you know, but what G. Stein once said about Oakland is what you'd say about Ira.

What with the noise and the music and the beer, it wasn't long before some relatives from across the Rio came over and joined the party. Segundo de la Cruz was among the first to arrive and also among the first to ask about you. (He asked what the party was all about and who 'the nervous chubby guy' was. Segu said he hadn't heard of Ira before the primaries; talk about your low profiles.)

I left right before sundown and in time to see Ira's smiling countenance on just about every telephone pole between Santana's ranchito and Klail City. That, cuz, is no mean drive.

Tomorrow morning, early, Noddy and I are going to look over some land west of Klail; it's the old Cástulo Landín property. (The old Landín-Ledesma grant, remember?) It now belongs to Old Italo's boy, Tadeo, and we're talking of a quarter section that Noddy's interested in. Since I'm the Chief Loan Officer, I'm to handle the affair, and here's how it works: we (the Bank) buy the land, but we hand the money over to Tadeo, as a 'loan'; he pays interest on the loan twice a year (it's his money and ours, see?). Tadeo doesn't lose and the I.R.S. (one of their own fine laws) doesn't collect a penny: Why? Because Tadeo pays interest twice a year as per terms of the contract (40 payments) and then the Bank (ready?) *rents* the property (as holder of the first lien) and divides the 180 acres into 4 *labores* of 45 acres each to whomever wants to farm them. Now, Tadeo then has money in *deferred* payments as operational capital (on demand if he wants to, which he will not). To add to this, *he* can then rent the property back from the Bank, and *then* pay interest on this and on the 'loan' (both of which are deductible). What else? Well, he gets to keep his share of the Govt. money for not planting the sugar cane he wasn't going to plant in the first place. The icing: in two/ three years, Tadeo can default, and the land goes to the Bank (first lien) or to some *other* interested buyer who can then submit an offer (as little as $100 over the original asking price, and so on). Small potatoes for IRS, of course, but they'll close this hole if one gets *too* greedy. So where does the money come and go and then increase? On *credit*, that's where. Ah.

It may sound bad, evil maybe, but it's perfectly legal for now and 'under the existing Tax Code' as we say.

And the Texas Mexicans? Well, we're learning a bit here and there. Since you left, for examp., at least four new Texas Mexican real estate offices have opened up from Jonesville to Edgerton.

And, some of the younger guys just out of college & law are ganging up and buying some of the old lands that had been lost years and years ago. Our Fellow Texans are sitting on top of the pile of money, but time will tell if they stay there.

With all this, however, one of Alinsky's phrases keeps coming up; now that the raza is *beginning* to wheel and deal, 'they'll all probably turn out to be shits'.

It's almost midnight, and Noddy'll be here fairly early.

                                        Best,
                                        Jehu


PS   What happened to the photo you promised? It wasn't enclosed; send it.

# 9

Dear Rafe:

The photo, and thanks.

Who's the girl? A Valley type? Looks half-Mexican, half-soldier. A beauty.

The preliminaries in re the land deal are well on their way; they're now in the hands of our attorneys, as we bankers say.

The return trip with Noddy was something, though. Looking straight ahead, even-voiced, he talked of his early times in the Valley. It's the fruit tramp for a father that gets him; it isn't shame, it's more of a resentment that some people haven't forgotten where he came from. I think that most people don't even know, but *he* knows, and you know how *that* goes. Even talked about his wife; he loves her, that's plain enough. It may be that *love's* not the right word, but he *cares*. It comes through.

He also cares about money, of c., but he likes to smell something out, haggle over it, 'jew 'em down, Jehu, and then he loves to mix it in with the lawyers and such. But, first, last, and always; politics. The man lives and breathes by it.

He has no time, won't give it, really, to the Rotarians & such. 'That's bullshit,' he says, but he'll send Ned Reese as a member, and pay his dues, too. Now, if the Kiwanians or the Lions need/want something, the Bank'll buy fifty tickets and no questions asked. And, of course, a steer here and there for the occasional barbecue.

As you so well know, Viola Barragán's good and opportune word played a fair part in my moving from the Savings and Loan right to the Bank, but I do earn my daily bread and no doubt on that score. He talked a bit about Viola; admiringly, almost. My *personal* life is my *personal* life he reminded me, and although he knows lot more than he lets on, he doesn't know *everything*. And, I didn't volunteer a word.

Veering off a bit here: He says I'm a born banker; that I was made for this job. (But: To die here, on this job? Gives one pause. Beats the hell out of teaching Eng. at Klail High, though.)

Speaking of Viola, as I was just now, I spotted her at one of Noddy's parties 'ta other night. It was held near the old Relámpago property. (Do you recall that land owned by the McCoys and the Ridings? Some Malacara kin (Chuy, Neto, and Gonzalo) bought some of it back and Noddy got the other half; both halves face the River). OK, there was Viola; she sees me, gives me a big, *big* hug, and says, 'Howza 'bout you 'n me gettin' together, Studley?' She's incorrigible, and we both burst out laughing to the surprise of our fellow-moochers there.

Don Javier L. was there, too. He must have thirty years on her, right? Anyway, Viola nudged me again and said, 'See that old fraud? He hiked himself on over to Houston for a special operation: he had a thin plastic tube inserted in his peter-nola; helps him pee, see, and he used it to bed whoever his latest is.'

She then mentioned Ollie and me; said it was a good thing I was thinking of settling down. She sends you her best and asked for your address; plans to send you a gift or two, I imagine.

Our old boss and now her present husband was lurking about and staying out of everybody's way; Viola B. keeps a very short rein. Rations, too, I would suspect. (*Old* Harmon *looks* old).

Viola and I mostly talked about Bank business. She's planning to buy some drive-in theaters (give 'em what they want, she says). She's a preferred customer at the Bank, but I said we'd still have to check her collateral. She winked right back and said, 'What I want to know, you sack full o' bones, is: when are you and I going to run-off together?' With this a kiss and a hug, and a reminder in re the drive-ins; she bustled off to mingle and have herself a hell of a good time. As she says, 'that's why parties were invented, goddammit.' "Go-demet" is how she says it.

What could I possibly add to VB's biog?

Olivia came up with two drinks in hand; she passed one on to me with the news that Becky wants to recommend her for the Woman's Club. (Back to *that* again). Ollie's nobody's fool, and Becky simply can't understand why someone wouldn't jump at the chance of joining the W.C. (They don't use the initials, I don't imagine).

For the record: of all the women at the party, and there was a bunch, Becky was the only one wearing a hat. She can flat-out wear one, too. Made her even better looking, and that's saying something.

Ira joined us, and what do you think he talked about? You win. And, what if he should lose, you ask? Let me say this, One: the

Valley mexicanos are convinced that Ira's their man. Two: the Anglo Texans know he's their boy. Money is bilingual, kid.

Here's a mild surprise: Morse Terry was in the bank this morn. He still does business with us. Noddy, to me, and in strictest conf., says that Morse is getting what's coming to him. Matter of factly; no heat.

(The party was the usual electioneering type of party: Anglo politics, Mexican food, Texas beer. We're both getting old, the parties and I.)

Signing off.

Best,<br>Jehu

# 10

Dear Rafe:

Primaries, primaries, o' when will they end?

The mexicano campaign manager for Ira is, need I say it?, none other than Polín Tapia. Polín slithered in quite early this a.m. to pick up 1) orders, and 2) money from Noddy: nihil novum.

Polín's still a youthful type; the years seem to pass right over him, and so do hints and direct insults, it would seem. All's well with his world, I guess.

Years ago when you and I were about twelve-years-old, (and I worked for Javier L. then), Bobby Campbell asked me if we considered Polín Tapia to be the Mayor of Mexican Town.

Fool that I was, I said, 'No, we don't'. What a dumb fuck I was in those days; we just weren't adept at fielding subtle insults, were we? Anyway, I remembered the 'Mexican Town' term, and I wondered what our Fellow Texans called the other mexicano neighborhoods such as Rebaje, Rincón del Diablo, Colonia Garza, etc.

Speaking of Campbell, in case you've any interest, he now works at a Sporting Goods Store in Edgerton. So much for being voted the one most likely.

Ollie and I are going to Barrones, Tamps., for the weekend. On the town. More (or less) on this at a later time.

It's a bit late, and I've got to call a halt here. Oh, before I forget: could/would you kindly call on a Wm. Barrett family for me, for old times' sake? I spent a week with them when I was getting my disch. papers at Fort Ben. They're named Gamboa and they live, or did, on Lake Street. Look 'em up.

> Best,
> Jehu

# 11

Dear Rafe:

Wednesday night.

You said there was more than met your jaundiced eye in the pre-primary goings on. Now, do you know something or is it merely our mutual paranoia? (PARANOIA: an independent disease which may be found present in the most intact of personalities). It's poss. that I'm too close to the action to be able to sit back, to analyze, etc.

Live and learn, I say. (Yes, Señorita Parker, it *is* National Cliché Week already): Becky was in early last Monday a.m. with an invitation to dinner at *her* house. A smallish affair. We're getting along, Mrs. Escobar and I, and I do so by putting on my best manners, my best foot forward, and my best face, too.

She hasn't got a kind word for *too* many people, I'm sorry to report. What she needs is a bit of balance, but no complaints from this end. She'll ask a personal question now and again, and I always trot out the truth. No reason not to, I say.

Noddy knows she asks questions, of course, but Noddy also knows me and trusts me not to go telling everything we do round here. (It isn't hard to figure out old NP, by the way. All one has to do is to remember that 1) he's sharp as hell, 2) he's got a mind like a sealed box, and 3) he can nail anybody he wants to. Anytime.)

So, there you have it. Things at Chez Escobar are in order with money in the bank, friends in the street, and votes in the bag.

As for Ira, he's got Washington, D.C. on the brain. (Becky does too, I'm sure of it). They're not even thinking of an apprenticeship up in Austin. No, sir. From Belken to Washington, but, as you say, first things first, and they are going to have to win the county election first of all. (Someone at the door).

Sunday morning. Sorry about the delay. Ollie came in, and we had a quiet dinner at home. On Fri., we went to the sit-down dinner at the Escobar's.

What now follows goes beyond conjecture.

From what Becky told me at the dinner, and from what I know, and from what I have been able to glue together, Morse Terry's decline and fall came about in this-here way:

It has to do with a certain business arrangement concerning FAMILY . . . Morse Terry, not here in Belken but rather in Dellis County, skinned some lands under Noddy's nose. It was a GOOD AMOUNT OF LAND, according to Becky. Morse was the broker for the opposing side; the opposing side in this case being a mexicano family from Flads right there in Dellis County. My *guess* is that it was the Cruz family or the Lermas or perhaps the Fischer Gutiérrez clan. Or all these, since they do work together well. At any rate, Noddy wanted that land for the Fam. What he *didn't* want, was for the land to fall into *those* mexicanos' hands. They're good, tough people and related to us on the Rincón side, right? Noddy knows this, but business is business. 'Them *cabrones* (Noddy here) are ganging up on me.' But he lost, and he lost well, I'll give him that; the anger had to wind up somewhere, and it devolved on Morse Terry.

To repeat: what I've sketched here is partly what B. said, and what I put together. She spoke rather emphatically, in confidence, and in the relative safety of her own living room. I, small time cynic that I am, asked myself, 'Why is she telling me all of this?' But, I've decided she enjoys passing information left and right. Ollie didn't say a word during all of this since she fell asleep a little after midnight. The talk went on till one or two. Becky, by the way, does have brown eyes; something like coffee sans creme. Great legs, too, or have I said that before?

Must close a bit sharply here, sorry. You're up-to-date on the latest.

Best,
Jehu

# 12

Dear Rafe:

Good to hear from you. Looks like you're coming along, and here's hoping you'll be home before the end of the year.

Some ticklish news here: On Sat. morn., the day after the visit to Chez Escobar, Morse Terry's wife was collared by none other than Patrolman Bowly T.G. Ponder; gave her a ticket, & a summons as well as a hard time during the writing of the citation. Yes, he did. *And*, yesterday, Mon., two of MT's accounts made an 'alienation of accounts' and transferred their business to Gaddis and Gaddis, Attys.-at-Law. Well now, MT isn't going to die of thirst or rabies on account of this, but it must be recognized that he has lost some ground here. As for his wife's arrest, why, that's just good old-fashioned harassment, pure and simple, as we know it in B. County. Judge Pike will mete out justice there.

And looky here: yesterday, still Mon., from out of left field somewhere out there, a new political opponent v. Terry. Another independent, they say: an Anglo, of course, from either Bascom or Edgerton, and brought in for that very purpose. This comes on top of Ira Escobar's resolute opposition which means that MT's going to have to come with some more cash; what we bankers call 'an unforeseen cash flow.' (Ira, by the way, isn't sweating the new guy in the race, and *that's* a surprise.)

Now then, if one adds this to the big money being spent on Ira, you and I have to admit that there is more to this than meets these tired old eyes. It's too much money for one piddling county seat, son.

But, as said, it's conjecture plus facts, and I have damn little hard evidence. Still, and this you can't deny, we both know which direction the raps are coming from, and, most importantly, who's doing the knocking. What is usually not known in these cases is when and how.

And here's the final entry in this grand historical design: our mutual former employer's printing shop misspelled — misspelled, for God's sake — Morse Terry's name. No, he didn't have to pay for their error, but why go on? The man then had to wait two (most prob. three) weeks for new plates, and by then, there were some new Ira Escobar signs all over the place. To add to this, Morse then had to wait an additional two or three days over the due date due to a shortage of ink. Shortage? In a printing shop? Of course, it could all be a great-big-huge monster of a coincidence. Of course.

Noddy tells me little or noth. (it being none of my business), and, besides, I'm just a hired hand. Officially, then, I know nothing.

Must close. Take c. of y'self.

Best,
Jehu

# 13

Dear Rafe:

To Relámpago and to Carmen Ranch; Israel and Aaron are doing well. In Relám. I visited Auntie Enriqueta who's ailing again; introduced her to Olivia or the other way round. Drove over to the old lands, and I got to see Angela Vielma and your sister-in-law Delfina. We gossipped about you a bit; Delfina wanted to know when you'd be marrying again; she says that a widower at 28 yrs. of age is prime material. Your sister-in-law looks happy as well she should after shedding the splendid Rómulo a couple of years back.

In case you're interested (and I doubt this with all my heart), Rómulo is still an uncivil servant at the Jonesville International Bridge. He's no longer family, of course, but from what the girls say, he drops by now and then. I remember how well you two got along.

From Relámpago, Ollie and I followed the river road to the Y that serves as the Flora-Klail City divider. We decided to go to Flora, and, needless to say, we saw and saw and saw Ira's smiling face all the way to Flora, which is not even one of the precinct towns.

Dinner, music, a little reading, and so to bed.

Best,
Jehu

# 14

Dear Rafe:

Three weeks plus some days before election time and counting.

First thing this morning at the office and what do I see (comin' for to carry me home)? A note on my desk:

Jehu: As soon as you come in,
come by the Ranch. Bring your brief case
& mine. Tell one of the girls to call
ahead that you're on your way.
                    N.

Said and done.

Trip takes some 30 minutes, and when I got to the Big House: nothing. Turned left by the show barn, and sho' nuff, some eight cars and pickups in front of the long bath house behind the pool and the bar.

I pulled in there at quarter to nine or so, and the cowboys must've been working on their third or fourth pot of coffee by then. And guess who was there? Morse Terry, that's who.

It was all cordially correct, if not exactly warm. I didn't know if I were there to act as pallbearer or what, but in I walked and handed NP his brief case, sat down, was served some coffee, and was then offered a cigarette.

Strange. It wasn't exactly the way *you* described what would prob. happen in that last letter of yours, but it came down close enough.

I'll back up. This last weekend, Ollie and I, as you know, drove up and down on both sides of the River and so I was out of pocket. It seems that Morse was squeezed some more between Fri. & Sun. The upshot of that piece of *bidness* is that Morse, hat in hand, came to see Noddy. At the Ranch, not at the Bank.

Now, as chief loan officer, and thus an officer of the Bank, I usually give one of three yea/nay votes, and hence my presence here:

it's a loan for MT; good-sized loan, as we say.

Mise en scéne: quiet on the set, and the only noise once in a w. is the one made by Sammie Jo's dive as she cuts through the water in that heated pool of hers. The loan is for $67,000 for six years at preferred loan risk rates, but with a king-sized collateral.

Some ass-holish hanger-on was going to be the so-called co-signer; a direct insult to MT. I suggested someone else; Noddy shot me a glance, and I pointed to Meredith Bohlen of Bohlen, Insurance. He's now the co-signer, and that was that. Papers in order & into my brief case, and I got my second cup of coffee for being such a nice boy at the hanging.

People moved around, shuffled about quietly, and when I looked at Morse (who must be around our age), he looked ten to fifteen years older, and who wouldn't? Noddy applied the make-up, set the scene, and steered the direction. As Noddy told me later on the way to the Bank: 'It's no mystery, Jehu; it's all very simple.'

That weekend, from Fri. p.m. to Sun. night, some 48 hrs., MT rec'd twenty, count 'em 20, telephone calls from clients & friends whom he represents as an atty. They'd been thinking, they said, quite seriously as it turns out, about considering another lawyer as their legal counsel. Nothing less.

Well, at the next-to-last phone call, it was suggested that 'he would do himself and all of us a big favor if he would call Mr. Perkins'.

Cave-in time. He called NP, and that was it. (The loan is merely Noddy's way of doing business, and you *were* right about MT dropping his pants and bending o.)

And there you have it, but as you prob. suspect, there's more. There always is, isn't there? Here it is:

Noddy wants Morse Terry in Washington. Ho-ho! Just Like That.

You see, at first I thought it was Noddy's revenge for that land deal I mentioned some time back or for past deeds & misdeeds, or hate, even. But no, it's been business all the time and when will I *ever* learn?

And will you look at this:

Noddy told me to stop at Cleo's Place for a drink and this at 10:30 a.m., mind you. NP was celebrating, and he wanted to fill me in some more. Our Congressman (whom you know well and whose niece Sophie you know even better) is still Hap Bayliss. Hap (according to Noddy) is ill: 'The man is dying, Jehu. You're one of the very few who knows just how sick he is . . .'

Could be. It could be that I'm one of the few, AND it could be that Hap really is dying. But, with Noddy you never know. Now, I do know some things I shouldn't, and now I wonder if Noddy knows I know . . . no, no, no, that way lies madness.

Two beers and a snack at Cleo's, & NP talked the while. Here is the rest of the Gospel acc. to St. Noddy who, by the way, is taking a few days off 'from all this.'

1) MT is to win Hap's seat; he'll do it as write-in candidate. That's right, and it's to be announced in good time. And this, then

2) paves the way for Ira's Commissioner's post (it also gets Ira out of the way) — But,

3) none of this gets out until Ira gets the biggest scare of his life. Bring him *more* to heel, as it were.

4) that, too, is Noddy's way of doing business.

While Noddy is going off on a short vac. he, naturally enough, won't be available to Ira.

Tonight, as I write this, there'll be some twenty calls to our boy (here we go again), telling him some people are planning to cross over to the independent side. Withdrawing their previous backing of I., see? Ira, of course, knows nothing of MT's recent conversion, and absolutely nothing whatsoever about Hap Bayliss and those designs. Plus, he hasn't been told of N's leaving town for a few days.

You can imagine the sucking of wind, given Ira's temperament and ASPIRATIONS. One more thing, Noddy's answering service will announce to please leave a message until Mr. Perkins can get back to the caller. (Hit me, said the masochist; I won't, said the sadist.)

So, Noddy'll be gone for the next three-four days.

New subject: am throwing away old letters, notes, papers, and the usual junk that's been piling up for yrs. and yrs. Few things will survive this purge. Not to worry, I'm fine; it's just a bit of overdue cleaning up, that's all.

Best,
Jehu

# 15

Dear Rafe:

Loan and Arrangement Day with Morse T. plus four. For all purposes, no official word in re the Bayliss-Perkins-Terry entente cordiale, and Ira is going out of what he is pleased to call his mind. The campaign posters are still up there, all right, and apparently nothing has changed. To top it, Ira told me yesterday morn. that Becky's gone to Jonesville for a few days (which I knew from her, of c.). But that's all Ira told me & he hasn't taken me into his confidence about the phone calls. (Neither did Becky.)

The election is now exactly two weeks off, and Ira thinks he's losing ground: he's not, but *he* thinks he is. Ira can't bring himself to ask me about Noddy, his whereabouts, or about his private line; Ira is in a bad way, and it promises to get worse. (For your information: Noddy had flown up to Wm. Barrett International to meet Hap B. Hap then flew back to Washington, and Noddy buzzed in late last night; he called and said he wanted to see me at the Ranch fairly early. He sounded happy, and that's always a bad sign.)

So, early this morning it starts again: I've been at the Ranch since 9 or so, a pile of papers for Noddy and me to sign when he stops around eleven and says (winking, mind you), 'Time to call Ira.'

He did and, believe me, I could hear Ira's heaving & breathing. Noddy begins by saying that he *just* got in from out of town and that there must be some one-hundred or more messages from Ira for him. Noddy's looking right at me when he says this, and he follows that with this: 'Hey, Ira, you're not thinking of dropping out of the race, are you?'

A dying groan from I., and before he can recover, Noddy the Splendid asks about Becky (knowing full well) and then he offers to send a Ranch car to pick up Ira at the Bank.

Ira's in no condition to drive and thus he waits there for the car that'll drive him straight into the lion's den. The driver must have taken the longer way home 'cause Noddy and I talked business, signed papers, ate a snack, drank a glass of beer, and Ira *still* wasn't at the Ranch. For all I know, Noddy planned it that way.

(Don't mind me; while I may not live in Paranoiaville, I *have* bought some land out in the suburbs.)

When Ira finally showed up, Noddy was all smiles; poor Ira didn't notice that NP was using that low voice of his.

Here, let me finish this up: Noddy sounded hurt; he said he'd heard that Ira was going round saying that he—Ira—didn't owe a favor to anybody; that he—Ira—had gotten to where he was on his own, by his own bootstraps. And then, in that low voice, Noddy said, 'Now that's what I call downright ungrateful, Ira.'

I'd say 'Poor Ira' again, but *he* wanted the job, right? Well, he got it, all right.

Noddy sat him down (literally) and talked about the importance of water rights in the Valley. How the water was apportioned in Belken County; who manned the irrigation ditches; who assigned the watering days and the amount, and when it was to be let out. Plain as Salisbury it was. Noddy talks about water rights, but Ira sits there and nods and agrees, and he still doesn't know that what N. is really talking about is pure and simple *control*.

Last entry: Noddy offered Ira a beer, and he took it; the man's allergic to beer, for Christ's sake!

Hold it. Telephone. It was Ollie; she's coming over.

Note: I don't think I'm going to last here much longer; I don't have the tummy for it. Ira may be a perfect fool, but he's still a human being.

Best,
Jehu

Confession time: I haven't been able to do what Noddy told me to do when he first hired me at the Savings & Loan: 'You're going to have to learn not to give a damn, Jehu. When you learn *that*, you'll be successful, but not before.' Man's right.

# 16

Dear Rafe:

It's a good thing I've got a private office at the Bank; and yes, I do enjoy a good laugh once in a while, but do exercise a little Christian charity, cousin. Your laughing, too, was music to these old ears; anyway, thanks a lot for the call. I needed it.

I may wind up dividing this one on an hour-by-hour basis.

Tuesday. Nine days to countdown

To being with: the write-in campaign (via radio and tv) is well on its way for MT who, as you know, is now going after Hap Bayliss's seat on Noddy's say so. Hap announced he was ill; it was on all the wire services, etc. I, too, will be less than charitable and say he got sick at Wm. Barrett International after his meeting with NP. One more thing for your kit bag: Hap, sick as he is, is leading the write-in campaign for MT. And that's how it's done: brown or not at all, and no q.'s asked.

The paid political announcements, a euph., can be seen and heard on every Valley station: in Eng. and in Spn. both. The stations spell out Morse's name, make no mistake says the announcer. Then, it's repeated and finally spelled out a third time. And, in order not to miss anyone (the deaf shall also vote) the name comes out ever so slowly across the tv screen as if announcing a Gulf hurricane or something. (Ira? He's in like a second-story man as Comm. Precinct 3, but he's dead to the world. He had the election in his sweaty palm, then NP came and took it away, and then NP came right back and handed it to him, but it was more than our boy could take. But, as you and I laughed about it this morning, it was MT for Washington all the time and all the way. We have much to learn.)

I'm telling you, and you heard it here first, he'll win big with Morse and the strawman out of the way, but NP squeezed what juice and flavor there were in that navel orange. And, of course, Ira knows nothing about anything. And he certainly doesn't know about

Beck and me. Period.

Morse, although he doesn't come round here much, is in contact with Noddy; NP told him not to be more than six feet away from the phone, and so our future Congressman is a prisoner in his own home. (In Washington, it'll be the same thing; as Noddy told him, in my office, 'We're just a phone call away, Morse.'

To touch lightly on what you said: Yes, you *are* right, I do know more than I should about some things, and, to repeat, you're *so* right when you say I have to take care.

One thing, though, I've no major debts to settle, nor do I have any pending accounts, to use the etymological root . . . *One* consolation is to know that NP can run me off when he wants to, but the *other* is that I, too, can walk away the same way I came here three years ago: one hand forward and one hand back, left-right-left, and right through that front door without dragging any shit behind me.

By the by, Becky doesn't rank among the very best; what she does offer is the well-known Mexican fury and flurry. No complaints, mind you, I thought it'd be a one-shot affair, but glad to report I was wrong.

Turned the radio on just now. Ho-ho! They're flooding *all* the stations again, and on both sides of the River, too.

Tonight's the last rally for the Klail mexicanos' vote. A form of insurance, let's say. There'll be further instructions on the spelling of Morse's name, although five'll get you that ten that the elec. judges will count *anything* that resembles MT's name. And, as the Father Confessor once asked; 'Is this the first time, my son?'

Mr. Polín Tapia, who else? is the head cheerleader tonight. And *that*, cousin, is how the system works around here; as if I had to tell *you* that.

Oh, and before I forget: no Texas Rangers at the polling places. A sign of the times, say the optimists, a sign from Noddy, say I.

To something else. Today, Sanford Blanchard showed up at the Bank. 'The Terror of the Female Household Staff' rushed right into Noddy's office as I was walking out. I looked to Noddy in case he needed help, but a shake of the head got me out of there. Sanford is a Bank Director, by the by, but he always votes by proxy. Sidney (Sammie Jo's No. 2, as y. know) stayed in the car while Sanford came to see Noddy. Some trouble or another at the Ranch, I expect.

Sanford prob. can't get it up much these days, but in his younger days he was a dangerous species: he could outrun and catch any Mexican, Nicaraguan, or Guatemalan maid brought out to the Ranch; a lot of shit in that Ranch, cousin, and like it or not, I'm a part of it. But, in your heart of hearts, do you believe that some of *our* friends would give me a job if I were to need one all of a sudden? Aside from Viola, they didn't do it back then when I needed one. And now? Well, I'm not buying three pounds of shit in a two-pound bag. Neither you nor I, Rafe, owe 'em a whole hell of a lot:

'fools and knaves

at the breakfast table. . .'

You're prob. laughing, right? But that's it, son. The mexicano people can also be ass-holish when it feels like it, and I'm fresh out of brotherly love. Old-fashioned class and shame have just about played out in Belken County. Think not? Just wait for the gnashing of teeth when the word gets out that you *gave* Acosta that land for $10. total. They'll call you a fool, our friends will.

Don't pay too much attention to me, it's just me and the Curse. Look, if there's something tomorrow or the day after, I'll call or pass it along; if not, I'll wait until I hear from you.

Best,
Jehu

# 17

Dear Rafe:

And what has happened in the last six days or so? Noddy damn thing, as we say. The radio & tv ads are still in absolute and full swing. Morse is still at home plate (we're as near as your teleph.) and Ira is one shaken young man. (Becky called; she's now the Pres.-elect to the Woman's Club. How is *that* for a surp.? She was presented with a silver platter, she was, and with honors too numerous to mention, and *yes* I saw her again. Can't be helped when you're young, you know.)

Ira can't believe he's got the election in one of those pockets of his three-piece suit; he still thinks *something's* going to happen. Noddy doesn't know how good a job he did on Ira. WHAT AM I SAYING? Of *course*, he knows. He just enjoys seeing Ira hop, is all. . .

The elections, and there must be another word we could use, are two days away.

On a personal note. Have not seen Ollie in 5 to 6 days; and she's not returning my calls at the pharm. It isn't as if we're formally engaged (is that still done?), but I (at least *I*) thought we had something serious there. Unless Becky blabbed; I take that back. Still, where there's smoke, right?

The phone just rang. Sammie Jo; wants to talk. In person. I'll continue this mañana.

J.

Here I am again. SJ's worried; thinks Uncle Sanford knows about our get-togethers. She's not *that* worried, but she's thinking of me and the job at the B. About her Dad, I imagine, and what he'd do. Told her that Sanf. had been at the Bank, but also told her not to w. Sanford Blanchard is hardly a reliable witness.

Tomorrow is election day (and I'll be glad when that's done). Bayliss (yesterday or the day before) announced he was a *vurry* sick man and gave his unconditional imprimatur and nihil obstat to MT. (Just one more time for those who didn't get it the first twenty times or so.) Bonus: we now have video tapes in many of Klail City's business estabs. & you can enjoy pro-Terry ads all you wish. We've two at the Bank, one in the coffee lounge, and one right smack in the middle of everything where Hap endorses his young, talented, and long-time friend. Endlessly. And, speaking of Morse, he called on me this morn.

Ready? He wants me to go to Washington with him. To work in his DC office! Noddy's move, I'm sure. Bribe? Could be. Spying on MT? Most prob. Anyway, I did thank MT, but no, thanks.

And so it goes round here. Still no word from Ollie; I call, leave my name and no., but silence reigns.

Long day tomorrow. You getting any better up there?

Best,<br>Jehu

# 18

Dear Rafe:

Election Day plus two and God's in His heaven, and Noddy's in his, regarding each other with suspicion, one would imagine.

Well, sir, it's in all the papers, and I'm not telling you something you don't already know. And now, it's simply a matter of picking up the pieces and the litter.

Our newest commissioner is more restrained, less exhuberant, *as it were*. This last is now a pet phrase. As such, he uses it at the drop of a jaw. If he's not careful, the instructed electorate will start calling him *Asitwere*. At the very least.

Two days in office, and he's saying things such as 'early on', and 'within these walls', and 'the sense of the meeting' and on and on. There just may be a little black book with all of that claptrap, and Ira may just have committed it to memory. Speaking of memory, as I just was, it would appear that Ollie has dropped me from hers. And via the U S Mail, too. Done struck out, Coach. And here I was, getting serious for the first time in *years*. Goes to show you.

This p.m., around closing time, Noddy came by my office. A dinner invitation to the Big House (& bring a friend, Jehu). I guess the old sumbitch knows about 0. like he knows most things round here. Anyway, dinner's on for tomorrow night. Cocktails at eight; dinner at nine. Veddy formal. As you may supp., I can hardly wait.

Don't know who'll be there, but I can wager it'll be Ira and Becky, Morse and his wife (Bedelia Boyer; grateful Bedelia, as I remember you calling her). Don't know who else will be in attendance. NP said it would be a smallish affair for a few of us. Us?

Translation: Important to all concerned.

I'll see where I fit in. Cocktails at 8 and no masks, but with Noddy, who's to know?

Hang on.

Best,
Jehu

# 19

Dear Rafe:

Just called you, but as always, nothing doing, and so I'll write. (I also called you last night after *the dinner*, but no answer. May I ask just what the hell kind of a hosp. they're running up there where no one answers the ph.?)

Some *dinner*.

Here we go: *The table had been picked and cleared by the time I got there.* I got there at eight, on the penny, and I spent three minutes at the Big House in all; tops.

Becky didn't raise her eyes (the whole time), the Terrys bit their respective lower lips (no surprise there) and Ira studied the Utrillo on the wall (an art lover, yet).

Noddy made it short: 'Jehu, I recommend that you resign as loan officer.'

I didn't say a word; the shock, needless to say.

I also left with my tail between my legs. To home and to worry, of which I did some on the way there. And I *did* worry, until — damn my eyes! — I *stopped*. I was doing exactly what Noddy wanted me to do; expected me to do. Go home and worry. About the *why*. Oh, he's a bastard all right, I'll give him that. (Note: he said *loan officer*; not from the *bank* itself. Now, what did the *others* hear?

Resign as loan officer and then what? Be demoted? Would I then stay? And, if I did, would I then be cooked? If I left, I'd be out of a job, sure, but there's always Viola. Another alternative: the Savings & Loan, but I wouldn't go back there at the point of a gun.

Noddy, aside from being a bastard, as said, is also a very good teacher, and I'll give him that, too. Maybe I'm his prize pupil.

Going to bed, son; tired and whether I want to admit it or not, shaky as Hell. I didn't think I'd mind leaving the Bank, but he's some kind-a bastard.

He did it in front of everybody. Ha! That's it, Rafe! He didn't do it *alone*; he *couldn't* do it alone. But that's been his pattern all along . . .

I bet, I just *bet* that Ira & Becky and the Terrys were just as surprised (shocked) as I was. They were told dinner was at six, say seven, and so, by eight . . . Jesus!

So? Look at this: day after tomorrow, to the Bank, as if nothing's happened. Monday is Armistice Day, and thus a bank holiday; I'll try to call you again and get more of this on the phone.

Good night, R.

Best,
Jehu

# 20

Dear Rafe:

The rub (a dub-dub) as Shakespeare and don Víctor Peláez used to say, was the coming out of anything smelling mighty but lak-a-rose. To walk out of that Bank would look (and smell) bad, and, added to which, I'd have a hell of a time explaining it; I did what I *had* to do.

I went to Noddy's office (as usual) and upon closing the door, I told him I wanted to go back to the Savings & Loan (which must've surprised him) but I needed a topic to start on.

'It's out of my hands, Jehu.'

I said it wasn't, and he said it was. I then said it'd look like hell (for me) if he let me go like that.

'You brought that on yourself, Jehu.'

I didn't argue the point 'cause if I did, we'd get into this, that, t'other, and I'd lose there, no question.

There I was, holding a Chinese straight and nothing else. Arms crossed, and looking straight on, I said: 'Does my firing have anything to do with sex, Noddy?'

Well! He squinted those faded old blues (one of his favorite ploys that squint) and *then* he exploded:

'You Mexican son-of-a-bitch!'

But I was ready. Ten, maybe even five years ago I'd-a knocked him on his ass for that, but not now, not this time. What I did, was to walk across the room, sit, look straight at him, and say: 'You may as well hear it straight from me: Becky and I had a couple of tussles, but that was it.'

'Becky? Who the hell said anything about Becky Escobar, goddammit!'

And I: 'Then who the hell *are* you talking about? And it sure as hell better not be Ollie, 'cause that's *my* business and not the bank's, goddammit.'

'Ollie? San Esteban? I'm talking about Sammie Jo, you son-of-a-bitch!'

'Sammie Jo? You've got a-hold of some bad shit there, Noddy.'

'*Bull*shit!'

'Bull*shit*. Let's call her, better still, let's go on out there, goddammit.'

'You . . .'

'Hold on, Noddy. You *know* I'm telling the truth . . . It's something *else*, isn't it?'

The man was absolutely right, of course. But, he was bluffing; the man had aces showing, all right, but he had *shit* in the hole.

NP knows me, and he knew I was going to come over to the Bank. I swear it. But I was ready for him. This time.

And he went on:

'You gonna make a speech?'

That old fart was still swinging away, back against the wall and full of fight.

'No,' I said. 'I'm no capon, but I'm not a goddam fool, either.'

I turned to go when he said, 'You know it hurts like hell.'

'Bullshit, Noddy.'

'Okay, okay; let me start over: so you and Becky . . .'

'Sure, twice; maybe three times. I don't remember.'

'Don't *remember*?'

'No! Who the hell counts? Look, Noddy, I haven't done anything you wouldn't have done at my age. But you're wrong about Sammie and me. We're close, and we've known each other since high school, but that's it, goddammit!'

'Is that the speech?'

The old son of a bitch won't ever let you go.

'And one more goddammed thing: we'll get into that Mexican son-of-a-bitch thing at another time.'

'Oh, yeah? And what makes you think you're still working here?'

'Well, you haven't thrown me out yet.'

And with that, the old sumbitch laughed, and that's the *closest* he'll come to an apology.

So, it's settled. I'm still the chief loan officer, and that's that.

Of course, he now knows about Becky and me, but I must say this: when he learns (for a fact) 'bout Sammie Jo and me, then it'll really be my ass.

Wanna bet?

Best,
Jehu

# 21

Dear Rafe:

Thanks for the call and thank you for the congratulations. Experimental evidence has shown that congratulations when dealing with NP must wait some five to ten years. Man's got a long arm to go with that memory of his.

Now that I think back on it, Sanford and Sidney must have put a flea in Noddy's ear. And why was Sanford the messenger boy? Because NP can't stand his own son-in-law. (And thanks for the tip.)

This a.m. (when you're hitting for extra bases, it's best to swing from the h.) I told Esther to hold all calls: I walked to the pharmacy and went to see Ollie. I had to.

It's on between us again, but on a different footing. I told her about Becky *and* about Sammie Jo, and that's how serious *I* am.

Things are back to normal: Ira carries on his share of the gloat by crossing each *t* and by dotting each *i*; he used to do it the other way round, but Ira is nothing if not compulsive.

Noddy's up in Colo., went to pick up Mrs. P. and taking some time off, too. The bank's rocking along and so's the work here. I'm thinking about leaving in a couple of mos. May go up to see you, may go up to Austin, may do both. Grad Sch. looks better every day, and I'm close to 30 yrs. of a.

When I do leave, though, I'm really not planning on anything def. for a bit. But I'll leave, that's sure, and under my own steam and terms. This time.

Poor Ira. Sees me here, and he doesn't know what to do or think. Talk about not believing your eyes.

In re Sammie Jo. It's over for a while. More importantly, we're still friends. As always. As for Becky: no comment. She's now busy with the Music Club, yes, that too, and now we're out of each other's hair, as it were. And, I guess that when Beck and I are both sixty years old, we'll look back on this and laugh about it. I can hardly wait.

VB then lit a cigarette and said, 'We need a business manager. Any time you want to chuck this place, let me know; pronto. Gotta go, now. Oh, before I do forget: I want a personalized wedding invitation, hear?'

No idea where she heard *that*. Not a bit of truth to it. Cross my eyes.

This much is settled: Ollie and I'll go up to see you in Wm. Barrett. That's still on.

Best,
Jehu

# 22

Dear Rafe:

Eine feste Burg ist unser Klail; impregnable, too. When I tell you that I see this town of ours, and I can't believe what I *do* see, then it's just too much, even for me.

The election doings provided the temporary bread and circus, of course, and people round here talk of nothing else. Complaints, mostly, but only after all has been said and done.

String's playing out, though. Came home after work, had myself a beer, & went on another cleaning binge. Whatever survived the last purge, didn't survive this one.

It's funny how I've accumulated all kinds and manner of trash, and particularly since discarding is more in my line.

To the basket one and all; out, damned spots. Took some three hours, maybe more, and I did count some dozen or more grocery bags full of junk. Junk which wasn't 'junk' then, of course. Clean slates. Can't begin (may not want to, in fact) to explain how this came about. First I threw away this picture and then that letter and then that one, and it was easier every time. Therapy is what it is.

I'm up to here and there with the elections, the shit, the talk, the etc. and the etc. too. Staying in tonight and tomorrow night, and the night after that. Plan to read and re-read. Ollie may come over; I don't know. She's the best, really; but for a lifetime? Time will tell.

Also, there must be something else other than that slow, winding road to Our Lady of Mercy cemetery. There must be.

All of this on one beer? Not to worry, nothing serious. This, too, shall pass.

Don't, not for one minute, think that this has anything to do with your letter or with the visit up there. I needed that visit, and I needed to be with Ollie more than just overnight. I'll be okay.

Best,

Jehu

# 23

Dear Rafe:

Israel and Aaron parachuted in on me last weekend. I'm sure you put them up to it, and thanks. I didn't know I needed the company. Friends are fine and a woman is better, but you can't beat relatives.

I *was* glad to see them; they sat down, smiled, and said I was under arrest: going for a three-day sentence to Carmen Ranch for hunting and fishing, they said. I went along meekly, and I had a hell of a good time.

From my apt. window facing Hidalgo and First, I can see half of Klail, but only when I want to; I'm better now, and I'm about to decide.

This is the end of my second three-day pass away from the Bank; I'll take three days off again next week and then couple them with the weekend. O. and I are going to the beach for four or five days.

There's the phone again.

Gotta go.

Best,
Jehu

# Part II

# P. Galindo

# 24
# Polin Tapia

Of the same military class as the wri, they have known each
other for years. Of Polín it was once said (by don Abdón Bermúdez,
from most accounts) that one would do well to count one's fingers
*and* nails after shaking hands with Polín. Don Abdón's phrase, a bit
short on charity, may not be too far off the mark, according to the
regulars at the Blue Bar.

Tapia lives off politics and such, and thus some mexicano Klail-
ites don't care for him. On the other hand, Federico 'Chancla' Ruiz
does the same thing, and is considered *simpático*. This may be set
down as differences in style.

The wri (equality among men) is all ears: the wri, content to
find a source of information, will be happier to judge later on. For
now, equity and discretion is his motto.

"Where to start, Galindo? Are the elections as good a place as
any? Let's see . . . About the time Ira Escobar decided, definitely
decided, to run for the Commissioner's post, and by that time he'd
gotten the Ranch's and the Bank's backing, I volunteered to help in
any way, at any time. That's my style, see? You have to be on your
toes, you know. Anyway, you yourself know that I have a certain
flair, a talent, for this type of work.

"I've always got some favors to call in, and I do, and it's usually
a matter of 'I'll scratch yours and you scratch mine'. But what the
hey! Why am I wasting my time telling you this? You wrote the
primer, Galindo; you know as much about this as anyone. Right?"

The wri likes to believe that he is above accepting flattery and
heavy-handed compliments. Note: the wri is more than fairly ignor-
ant about many, many things, and it's been only recently that he
learned to admit how little he does know.

"Weeeeeeeeeeeeeeeeeell, Ira decides to oppose Morse Terry, a .400 hitter, Galindo, and one whom I also know quite well. Anyway, the fight's the thing, as the saying goes, but hard work and talent bring out the best in me, right?

"As you know, Ira won the generals in November; now, that Bayliss fell ill around that time, and that Morse took the Congressional seat as a write-in is something else again. I can hardly be blamed for *that*; I concentrated on the commissioner's race, right? This was my first priority, right? A-course, if I could see into the future, why, Ira'd be a Congressman by now, yes, he would. Cross my heart, Galindo. But a commissioner is a commissioner, and Belken's no down-at-the-heels county like Dellis, right? And like I always say, you got to start somewhere, hey?"

Self-corroboration is PT's strongest suit.

"The kids and the older folk at the bank worked like Trojans at election time. They stuffed envelopes, made telephone calls, raised a little money here and there, and like that. Stalwarts, all of 'em. But I'll tell you who didn't turn a lick; Jehu Malacara. I didn't *ask* him to help, but my God!, the way everyone else was hustling around there, why, you'd think he'd at least take a *hint*. God, no; thought didn't even occur to him. Hah! The only time he *said* something it sure as hell wasn't *constructive*; he told me it'd be best if I tried *working* for a living. Can you imagine that? *Him* telling *me* that? Is that what they teach 'em up in Austin? Is that the mark of an educated man?"

The wri has no idea how anyone is educated up there.

"Well! *I've* known Jehu since he was the sweep and clean up boy at the Chagos' barbershop. Humph! Has he forgotten *that*? Ha! I sure as hell don't tell *him* how to do his job at the bank, do I?

"Ira's something else again, though. He's got a sense of humor, he knows how to laugh, knows how to show a courtesy or two, and, and, here, let me tell you this: I even drive that big Olds a-his 'n that. Ha! And Jehu? Shoot! He doesn't even *own* a car 'cause that green MG's not his, no sir: that little car belongs to the pharmacist woman friend a-his.

"Look, in my opinion, Jehu is used to having everything come his way. Everything. Made to order. It's got to be his way, or he won't play. Humph. It's time he found out what *working* is all about. That's right.

"I'm not criticizing, Galindo. In politics one learns to evaluate, rate, okay? I'm not angry, no. And no resentment, either. You, as a writer and newspaperman, know all about this."

The wri insists to the reader that the wri doesn't know much about a lot of things.

"Jehu worked at the bank, was handed a post of *some* responsibility, he had a year or two of seniority on Ira, but Ira, on talent alone earned more money than Jehu; yes, he did. Ira told me so. And what happens when you open those double-doors to the bank? The first person you see is Ira, but where is Jehu? I'll tell you where: Jehu was stuck in some small office next to Noddy Perkins' big office, that's where.

"Ira's good people, Galindo. Yes, he is. And a nice guy, to boot. Why, you won't see *him* at the *Aquí me quedo Bar* or, worse at the Blue Bar. You'll see Jehu there, though; oh, yeah. Look, as a newspaperman *you* can go anywhere, any time. But Jehu? He's a banker! Geez! He was lowering himself, he was. And did he *care*?

"Oh, and as far as that laugh a-his, well, I'm not fooled one bit by that; no sir. That's plain old ridicule, is what that is. That's *right*. I mean, what the hell does he think he is, some sort-a royalty?

"Tell you what. My Dad, and my uncle, too, never — hear? — never hired Jehu at their place, because Jehu wasn't dependable nor serious, either. Nope. You got to work hard, polishing and wiping the furniture and the washing machines and what-all. 'A furniture store survives on shine,' my Dad used-a say. No, sir; Jehu wouldn't-a lasted a day there.

"Now, between you 'n me, I'm going to tell you something in absolute, strictest confidence: Ira may be a chubby sort, but he's All Man, yessir. Now, I know Jehu, and all I can say is that he's damn lucky he didn't set eyes on Becky or he'd-a been in big trouble, yessir. He doesn't know Ira Escobar, not like I do. Why, Ira'd made a capon out-a that boy, yes he would've. Ha! You don't think so?"

The wri, an agnostic, holds few beliefs.

"One thing for sure, people don't walk away from a cinch job every day o' the week. Nossir. I'm not saying that he was run off at the bank, but it doesn't look good his going away like that. Right? You be the judge."

The wri, no callow youth, caught himself (a time or two) with mouth agape. It'd be unnecessary to say that Polín resents Jehu somewhat, but no one's perfect, as Polín himself says. It should be understood, however, right here and now, that Polín is quite open in his assessments, in his preferences; he doesn't, then, hold anything back. That he says what he does say, may reveal the mutual confidence between PT and the wri.

But, this is what this is all about in the first place. The reader is to arrive at a personal conclusion and not wait for the wri to tie the noose round the ring to lead the reader by the nose. As it were.

# 25

# Ira Escobar

A co-worker of Jehu's at the Klail City First National, and new-ly elected first-term County Commissioner, Precinct 3. Married and thus wedded to Rebecca Escobar née Caldwell, Ira was not enthusiastic to speak to the wri at the Bank, at first. But (broadminded that he is) Ira came round to give his views in the Jehu Malacara affair.

"Sure, I know him well; I've, ah, I've helped him out a couple of times, or I did. He was the ch, chief loan officer, but he, ah, he needed help once in a while. And, what are friends for, as *I* always say.

"I can't say he was much interested in politics, though he read quite a bit; at least I always had the impresson he read quite a bit. Know what I mean?

"We never, ah, ah, seldom saw each other socially except for bank parties or at political barbecues. He didn't take the barbecues seriously; he, ah, he thought they were one big joke, you know. I really don't understand why Noddy (The wri noted that the deponent looked first to his right and then to his left), Mr. Perkins, Nod-dy . . . I don't know why Jehu was hired. I mean, he, Jehu, had a certain flair for this type of work but ah . . . talent? Now, as to . . ."

The wri waited until IE finished his sentence, but it was not to be. The sentence died on a sigh . . .

"We got along well, though. At first, my wife cried for him, but after a couple of times or so, she hardly mentioned him at all, and I don't believe she's talked to Jehu for the last eight months or so. Anyway, Becky, my wife, is, ah, usually, ah, pretty busy with her work at the Music Club, and she works late once or twice a week. And, I was busy on my own campaign, which turned out well, as you know. So, the two of us, Becky and I, didn't exactly snub Jehu; we just simply didn't see much of him, that's all."

The wri needs to break in here: it is entirely possible that Becky Escobar works assiduously at the Woman's Club and at the Music Club as IE says. Let he who is without sin cast the very first etcetera.

"As loan officer, Jehu saw more of Mr. Per . . . of, ah, Noddy, than I did; my desk handles the smaller loans and some automobile notes, as well. I guess you know that I'd only been on the job a short while when I was asked to consider running for Commissioner for Place Three. You *must* have seen my pictures, right? I mean, they were fairly well plastered all over the place from Jonesville to Edgerton (titter) and from Relámpago on over to Ruffing (smile).
  "I like politics; it's a man's responsibility, and it's also a way to do public service, don't you agree?"

The wri has precious few opinions which tend to favor politics and none whatever for politicians. This is merely one of the many faults readily admitted to by the wri.

"When Noddy, ah, (slight jerking movement of the head) informed me that Jehu was leaving, he, Mr. Per . . . Noddy, ah, didn't *exactly* offer me the senior officer's loan post, but he, Noddy, ah, did say that with my added duties at the county level, that I, ah, would be far too busy with that end of it to be *chained* to the chief loan officer's desk.
  "I think I could handle both, but it could be that the Old Man (one of those rabbit-like smiles), I mean, that *Noddy*, you see, is right . . . Still, I mean, if Jehu did it, I could too, *right?*
  "I'm not putting him down or anything, but I could handle the job. Sure.
  "As for Jehu, again, well, he, ah . . . he had a certain difficulty of expression; an impediment. You know what I mean? His, ah, his English was a bit weak now and then, and that would've held him back had he stayed on here. Definitely.
  "Look; I wouldn't mind talking to you some more on this, but I do have a luncheon date over at the, ah, the Camelot . . . right?"

Yes, the wri agrees with the reader: IE did not mention the dinner held at Noddy Perkins' some time back. The wri feels there is no need to return to IE for further information in the near future. Remains to be seen, that's all.

# 26

# Martin San Esteban

A pharmacist; a fellow student of Rafe's and Jehu's at The University; slightly older than his sister, Olivia. Martin was born in Klail City, he grew up in Edgerton, and married one of the Ycaza girls from Ruffing. He and Olivia are co-owners of Klail City Drugs.

"We go back a long way, Jehu and I. I'm talking before Austin, and before the Army even. Yep, Jehu's always been like that. As for Ollie, I don't think they dated this much up at Austin.

"He and Rafe lived in that crazy place off Guadalupe and 26th the last two years. I roomed with my cousin at Mrs. Lundquist's.

"Do you know my cousin? Juan? Santoscoy? Well, the four of us used to run together at the University some; but neither Jehu nor Rafe were much for dances.

"I remember the time Rafe and Jehu and some other guys made some beer, some home brew. They made it *right* in the room. My God, they must have made close to ten cases of the stuff. It was dark stuff; strong, too.

"Austin wasn't that big then, you know. You could usually run into Jehu over on the West Mall. His first year there, he lived in that house by Scottish Rite; and *that* was a madhouse, and I think all the guys there were communists. Jesus! Jehu *loved* it; Rafe usually sat there, drinking his beer, talking now and then. Most of the guys who lived there were from South America or Mexico, and Jehu, 'n don't ask me why, called them The Filipinos. They didn't seem to mind it, either . . . it was strange.

"Jehu was an English major; I'm not sure he was planning to teach, though. I'll tell you this, I had no *idea* what he was going to do with *that* degree. Juan and I were both in pharmacy and we knew we had a job; and, then, later on, Mom and Dad bought this place here.

"Ollie . . . Ollie's been dating Jehu some, and now she's got it into her head about going up to Galveston. I mean, she wants to *apply* to *med* school, can you imagine? Shoot, we've got business enough *here* already. And for two more pharmacists if we wanted to.

"But Jehu's like that, you know, I mean, no sooner did he get a job at Klail High than he started thinking about something *else*.

"He's lucky, though, I'll say that. He usually manages to land some pretty good jobs; he just doesn't stick to 'em, that's all. Why, look at the job at the bank; they *liked* him there, you know.

"And now Ollie says that Jehu wants to get a Master's degree. Well, what does one *do* with a Master's in English. I mean, he's already taught at the high school, and he could probably get another job there, but to go back to *that*? Shoot. The job at the bank *pays* better, and I just hope he didn't do anything there to screw it up. No, no, don't misunderstand, I'm not saying he did; I'm just saying that it wouldn't *look* good for the mexicanos if he did, see? But Jehu's *honest*. He's *crazy*, but he's honest.

"But like I said, he and Ollie go out once in a while. He was *hell* in Austin, though. But I'll tell you this: he won't get to first base with Ollie; she's a mexicana, and raised that way.

"Have you heard from Rafe lately, Mr. Galindo? He and I were kind-a tight up at Austin, for a while, but he's just *too* damn quiet sometimes. He's steady, though. Boy, he and Jehu made quite a pair; have you ever heard Jehu sing? I'm serious, yeah. He knows some *funny* songs. In *Spanish*. *He* could make Rafe laugh, out loud, too.

"Do you know Rafe's, ah, of course you do. I was about to ask if you knew Rafe's sister-in-law, Delfina. Well, Delfina was here the other day, and she said that Jehu had given her her grandmother's or maybe her great grandmother's, I'm not sure which, anyway, it was a bible. An *old* one. Rafe had given it to Jehu, and Jehu, about a week or two before he left last Fall, well, he gave it to Delfina. It's a nice old book, and probably worth a lot of money, is my guess.

"By the way, I've heard that Angela Vielma and Delfina have been talking about moving into that nice house off Palm View; the big one, the one that's kittycorner to Hidalgo Boulevard. You know, by the old school? It's a big house. And nice, too."

The wri had not met young San Esteban prior to this; he knew of him as he knows of a lot of other things in God's Littlest Acre: by chance. The wri has no commentary to make as to the pharmacist's views and opinions on Jehu; the wri thinks he detects a slight resentment at Jehu's seemingly carefree outlook, but the wri would also like to point out that he evinced no strong criticism of Jehu's ways. It could be that Martin simply doesn't understand Jehu, his ways, his ideas, or his sister's interest in medicine and Jehu.

# 27

# Viola Barragan

The wri is at a loss when it comes to explaining institutions, and VB *is* one. She's a firm believer in the *status quo ante*, of the American free enterprise system, a champion adherent of *laissez faire entre nous*, and a friend to her friends. She is also loyalty personified, an in-fighter, independent, brave, and a steady, resolute repository of all that is good and bad in the Valley. The wri (obviously, shamelessly) admires this *sui generis* personality.

"Well, Galindo! Long time and all that. Don't interrupt, I know, I know, you've been talking to people about Jehu's whereabouts, isn't that about it? Well, for starters, I can tell you right here and now, that that boy's got a job here whenever he wants one. Yessir. He's a hard worker, he's sharp, and, above everything else, a straight arrow. Plus, he's free to run my, knock on wood, many businesses here and there; they're doing well, knock with me, damn you, and that boy has a good nose for business.

"What can I tell you? You know me from way back and here I am, nudging fifty, and if you want to know something, just ask. You may not like what you hear, but the truth'll come out vanilla-clear, yessir.

"I talked to Noddy Pee-pockets about the boy not too long ago, and whatever else Noddy is, and he's a lot of things, there's no conning me: we talk shop, politics, you name it, and we talk straight. Every time. What I'm about to tell you, then, is less than a week old; I mean I talked to him then.

"He says that Jehu, some time ago, round election time, got to Becky Escobar. I figure that's nobody's business but theirs. And, if Noddy thought, for one damn minute, that I was going to blow *that* around here, then he sure as hell doesn't know Viola Barragán; not by a long damn chalk, hear? I'm not his goddam Western Union, nossir.

"Now, it's not that Noddy really gives a damn about that, but, what *I* didn't like then, and I still *don't*, dammit, is that Noddy said that Jehu may be in some sort of danger, or trouble, or peril, or something along that line on account of he pulled Becky's pants off. Heckfire, Galindo! They're old enough, right?

"Now then, what *I* wanted to know, and I talked to Noddy about this, what I wanted to know, was why he almost fired Jehu some time back. Oh, he tried, all right. I got this straight from Jehu. A shared confidence, you might say.

"All right, then, between you and me, too, Galindo. I'll bet, and I've no proof, okay? I'll bet Jehu got to Sammie Jo. That's right. The way I figure it, is that that's the main reason Livvie San Esteban dropped Jehu for a while. I'll tell you: the young have a lot to learn about a lot of things, and sex is one of them. Ha!

"I think, *think*, mind you, that Jehu is either at Carmen Ranch with Israel Buenrostro, and, if not there, then's he's up at William Barrett with Rafe. What's wrong with ringing in the New Year with his favorite cousin? You know those kids better'n I do; trouble is, you're not going to get Israel to tell you much, and neither you nor anyone else is going to get a word out of Rafe, and that's for damn sure.

"But, to repeat, if Jehu wants a job, he's got *me*. And I'll pay him a hell of a lot better than Noddy, and a whole hell of a lot better than my cheapskate husband. Fair's fair, is the way I see it.

"Now, it may or it may not mean a damn thing, but I haven't seen Javier Leguizamón's hand in any of this. That's no guarantee, though. I'd pay five-hundred dollars a ticket for a front row seat just to see that face a-his when they told him that Jehu pulled down Becky's underwe-ah, o' yeah! Pious old son-of-a-bitch; as if he hadn't diddled somebody in his day. Why . . .

"Look, Galindo, you yourself know, or you sure as hell should, that Javier himself got that dumb Ira Escobar's job for him. Yes, he did 'n I got *that* straight from Noddy; and as I told Noddy, to his face, too, 'See here, Noddy, when it comes to politics, you and I give money to all sides, and we don't much give a damn *what* party they come up with.'

"As for Ira, well, let me tell you this: Becky Caldwell married Ira Escobar for money, for the Leguizamón name, and because her Ma, Elvira Navarrete, wanted the Leguizamón union. Pure and simple. Sure, and then people talk about me whenever . . . Ha!

"Becky isn't a bad *kid*; oh, she likes a backroll now and again, and she does fool around with those Clubs and all, but she's her Ma all over again. Look who her Ma married: Catarino Caldwell, Caca. Proof enough? Do I know Elvira? Heart and soul, Galindo, heart and soul.

"And Sammie Jo? She flat likes it, and she's honest about it. An upfront kid, believe me. Married twice, you know: the first was drunk and then the second a bit of a drunk and a pansy boy, too.

"I got that last from Jehu. Gossip? Not a bit of it, and . . . What do you mean you didn't know?

"Here, lemme tell you: Jehu, on his way over to Sammie Jo's Ranch, there on the floor itself, found a chain, and it had one of those lockets on it, see? It was right by the pool. He didn't know whose it was; he picked it up and gave it to Sammie Jo. *She* opened it; she'd given it to Sidney, see? Well, sir, she opened it up, and there they were: two a-those small pictures, you know, cut-outs. One a-them was Sidney's, the other was Hap Bayliss's. Chew on that'n awhile.

"Know what Sammie Jo did? She shrugged, and then, she and Jehu went into her room and that was that. Tell you when it was: it was one-a the times Noddy was up at Colorado or up to William Barrett; I'm not su . . . yeah, I do: around election time it was.

"Jehu told me about it, but it wasn't gossip, mind you. Now, it's my guess that *that* was when he started to think about working over here, for me. You never can tell, you know; I mean, what if Sammie Jo, a drink here and there, sort-a lets it slip out about her husband and Bayliss, or about Jehu, right? A-course, she could have told her Dad right out, about the locket, see, and left out the other part. But I don't know this, I'm just talking now.

"About that time, too, though, Jehu and Livvie San Esteban were kind-a serious, or maybe even breaking up. One-a the two.

"The Anglo Texans can damn well do what they want to, and they usually do so in the Valley. What I *didn't* want, and what I still *don't* want, is for them to get Jehu chewed up in all-a their shit. Everybody needs a friend, and I'm here to protect that boy's interests. And, if he doesn't want to work for me here in Klail, he can well go to Dellis County where, thank the Lord, I've also got some businesses.

"And that's it, Galindo. What say you and I have a drink? But only one, 'kay?"

The wri before anything else, serves notice that that 'kay was followed by a healthy, well-meaning laugh on the part of Viola Barragán. The wri shared a tall glass of tea with VB, and the only thing he spent was time.

Difficulty: Viola Barragán does not lie, neither does she fabricate; she exaggerates very little, too, and she does stick to that which she knows. Despite these good points, the story does become somewhat complicated since Viola, with all of those good points in her favor, doesn't *know* if she knows everything. That aside, one should take what she says as gospel and not *cum granis salis*.

It's plainly evident that Viola is Jehu's champion. Affection and loyalty are to be treasured, of course, and Jehu is indeed fortunate in this regard. Fact: Jehu himself has always been straight as a dye with Viola Barragán.

# 28

# Bowly T.G. Ponder

A policeman in Klail City; he fills in as a traffic cop on occasion. Of medium build, on the thin side, a smallish flattened nose set on a ruddy face, and a shock of reddish brown hair, Ponder is a descendant of the poor whites who came to the Valley after World War I. The p.w. are on the lowest rung in the Valley's social ladder; the next to the lowest are the fruit tramps. Valley Texas Mexicans form no part in this social configuration.

Ponder was born in some of those lands bordering on the Ranch; his younger brother, Dempsey, works as a fence-rider for the Klail-Blanchard-Cooke interests; and he lives still in that same four-roomer where all nine Ponders were born; there are, then, a good number of Ponder relatives and in-laws strewn all over the Valley.

"Jehu? Sure; for years. He's a good guy; saved those two little kids on Vermont Avenue; that was about the time you was up at the V.A. Hospital. He didn't tell you about that?

"Yeah, he, ah, broke the rear windows of a car and got the kids out before they suffocated to death. Damfool woman'd left 'em in there to make a phone call or something, and the kids would've fried for sure.

"That was quick thinking on his part. Lessee . . . that happened during the primaries, about the time I ran-in Congressman Terry's wife for speeding. A-course, he was a commissioner then. You didn't know about either? Sure!

"Yeah, old Bowly T.G. ran her in; old Missy Stuck-up there was speeding, and I just up and gave her a ticket for it. I wad'nt about to take any crap from her. Anyway, I was just doing my job, is all.

"Know what? She told Judge Pike I was dis res pect ful. Little piss ant shit. I told *him* I expected the violator had been drinking some. Believe me, Galindo, I could've make that *stick* if I *needed* to.

"Know what else she said when I gave her the goddam ticket? She said I ought to go around checking on Mexican cars for state inspection tags if that was all I had to with my *time*.

"Piece of shit telling *me* how to do my *job*; well, I fixed *her* ass . . . I walked on over to my car, turned on the flashing lights, turned on the goddam car radio, loud!, and *then* I went back and *asked* her to get the hell out-a the car, to empty her purse, and wallet, too, and *then*, to open up the goddam glove compartment — from the outside — and then I made her walk around the car, too. Half-a-goddam Klail must have seen her; saw old John, you know, from the paint store? I waved to him, and then I *pointed* at her. Ol' John grinned and nodded at me.

"I don't give two hoots in anybody's hell; County Commissioner, *shit. He* speeds in Klail, *he* gets a ticket.

"And you know *what?* People round here are saying that Noddy sicced me on her; shoot! I don't mess with *his* bank, and *he* don't mess with *me*. Demps works for him, all right, but that's his and Demps's business — ain't none-a mine.

"And, to top it off, I had to take half a day off my vacation to go see Judge Fikes, too; and that's a fact, and she paid them twenty-two fifty right then and there. No two ways.

"Yeh, she was put out, all right. You know *what?* Betcha she don't speed in my sector again. And that's a *fact.*"

Mighty bold talk, but it happened, and let there be little doubt, that Bowly did tighten up some loose screws in Bedelia (Boyer) Terry's case. And, don't doubt that Bowly made some heavy tracks in Knowlton Pike's court that day.

With all that, however, the wri doth think that Bowly protests too much.

Working against Bowly's absolute credibility, and there's plenty of best evidence against him these past fifteen years, is the fact that he owes his post to Noddy Perkins (for starters). As a capper, his brother Dempsey works for the Ranch, all nephews, in-laws, relatives, etc related to the Ponders, and Bewleys, and the Watfell families, kneel at the same public trough.

That Bedelia Boyer Terry drives like a madwoman through some of Klail's streets is page-four stuff. That then, around election time, and for the first time ever, someone stopped her for speeding and then gives her a relatively hard time is too much of a coincidence.

The cat, then, pokes his head out of the bag there. The wri

needs to offer this piece of information since he can't sit there with his arms crossed knowing, as he does, a good part of the facts and the actors in this little drama.

# 29
# Olivia San Esteban

Willowy, supple and lithe all fit this mexicana beauty; looking at her, the wri calculates she's an inch or two shorter than Jehu, and not much more. Her eyes are brown as is her wavy hair; the wri hears a pleasant, clear voice, and, at twenty-nine and unmarried, she must be the envy of any number of Valley women. She laughs easily enough, but she's no giggler. The wri believes a further personal assessment of la San Esteban to be a true one: while no trimmer, she's not dogmatic, either; she claims she can speak on and about Jehu with no coloration of their personal lives. (The wri does not know how the personal can be avoided in this case).

"I knew of Jehu some time back, but didn't really meet him until we were up at Austin. He and Rafe would show up at some parties with my brother Martin and my cousin, Juan Santoscoy.

"It's no secret he was provided for by the Carmen Ranch Buenrostros. When Jehu orphaned early, they took him in; and, they're kin. Anyway, Jehu and I didn't go into that very much.

"He's headstrong about some things, but so am I; and yet, he and I agree on many things, too. One thing, though, our relationship is our relationship, and he won't take any guff from my brother Martin; right off the bat, too, he told Martin where to get off.

"He's like that.

"Now, Jehu and I do disagree on some things, as I said, but these are personal; and, speaking of personal things, just this once, Jehu is *very* much interested in my going to med school.

"I'm, ah, I'm just not *sure* he's quite ready to settle down, señor Galindo . . . Look, I'm really behind on some prescriptions and in the drug inventory at the moment. Could you come back later on? This afternoon?

That afternoon.

"Hello, and thanks for coming back like this; work's like that most mornings, but I'm off for the rest of the day now. Martin'll work nights this month, and if you're willing to wait till then, he may have something to add to Jehu's whereabouts. For my part, I'll say it's no great mystery: since he isn't at the Carmen Ranch, as you say, then he's either up at William Barrett or in Austin, one. I haven't heard from him this week yet.

"I don't know where to begin 'cause there's not much to say, really.

"The last name of Malacara misses the mark, doesn't it? He's not handsome or a pretty boy, but he's sexy, señor Galindo, and don't look so shocked.

"I now realize I know little about him. He told me he worked for some holy rollers once; those were funny stories, too, but then he could always make me laugh. But he's not a clown, you know what I'm saying? He smiles and laughs and all that, but he's serious more often than not, and, ah, I, I, I'm strong for him.

"What happens is that . . . look Mr. Galindo, I'm going to say something as clearly as I possibly can: I've no proof, but Becky Escobar not only let herself be caught, she did a lot of the chasing. I just know it; Sammie Jo, too, but I already know that. From him; he walked in here one day and said so, but he also said he was through with that. I believe him, Mr. Galindo.

"I'm not a kid; I'm twenty-nine, and I am the way I am: the way I choose to be, but I don't like and I don't want to share him, and I sure as *hell*, I *sure* as hell, don't want to share him with those two. And no, it isn't because they're married or anything like that. At all. They can run around as much as they please, but not with him. That's all.

"He's no kid, I know that; but the very same day he left the bank, he came *here*; he came to *see* me, and he came to say he was leaving for a while. He came to see *me*, in person. And I'll say this, too, while I'm at it, señor Galindo, he wasn't run *off* from the bank. That's right.

"Mrs. Barragán and I have little to say to each other, and it isn't enmity or anything like that; we know each other . . . where was I? Oh, yes; Mrs. Barragán offered him any number of jobs, positions, really. Any time he wants one, too. I know this from *him*, but, I know this from her. She told me so.

"As for me señor Galindo, I want to go to med school, and Jehu will help. I'm not talking about money, but he'd be a, a, a support. A mainstay. Yes, he would, and when he comes back, and he *will*, too, he'll come for me.

"And it doesn't matter whether we get married or not; he and I have this understanding. Oh, yes, I know about *people*, and what they say or *will* say, but I understand *him*, and you know what else? He understands me. That may not be much for some, but it's quite enough for me.

The informant did not, at any time, raise her voice. A stress here, an emphasis there, and that was it. She smiled a smile that resembles Jehu's, by the way. The wri would like to add that Olivia SE has a sense of the ironic, plus, she has a clear cut idea of who she is, as well.

The wri finds no need to add anything whatsoever to OSE's views and comments on Rebecca Escobar and Sammie Jo Perkins, since la San Esteban's views are quite definite in this respect.

Opinion: If anyone knows of Jehu's whereabouts, then it must surely be OSE, the wri thinks that the person who also knows more (perhaps all) is none other than Viola Barragán.

The wri feels he has to speak with Harmon Gillette's recent widow.*

---

*Olivia San Esteban refers to Viola Barragán as Mrs. Barragán; this is an error on her part. For the record: Viola née Barragán first married the physician Agustín Peñalosa, native to Agualeguas, Nuevo León, Mexico; he died as a result of an accidental, but nevertheless lethal, prescription handed to him by the apprentice Orfalindo Buitureyra.

Viola's second husband was the German Karl-Heinz Schuler, ex-diplomat to Mexico and India, and former representative of the Volkswagen Werke in Pretoria, South Africa. Herr Schuler died of a myocardial infarction; Viola returned to Ulm (Bavaria) and tended to her rather elderly in-laws for some seven-eight years until their respective natural deaths. Her third husband, also dead, of course, was the printer Harmon Gillette, of the up-river Gillettes. His death, from what the wri has learned, was a result of pancreatic cancer.

# 30
# Viola Barragan

Vide Nos. 27, 29.

"So good to see you again, Galindo. You're looking better these days; is it possible? Don't overdo it, now, get plenty of rest; you know how much we-all care for you.

"So? How are things going for you these days? Es ist immer das alte Lied?, as my Karl-Heinz used to say? Is it the same old tune?

"I really would like to stay and chat a while, but I'm up to my ears in work. I wouldn't be like this at all if I had a business manager like Jehu to run this for me. Here, open the door for me. That's it, thank you. Get the car door, too. (grunt) Thanks.

"Now, you be sure and call me when you hear somethin, 'kay? You really must excuse me, but I'm in a fightful hurry."

Supposition: But, is it possible that our Viola is avoiding the wri?

One answer: No, not necessarily; it could very possibly be that the multi-business affairs of this versatile woman are getting to be too much at times; too many and so much that although she would like to stop and chat, she can't.

Another: It is entirely possible that she just may be hiding something in that ample breast of hers.

Still another: She may be honor bound not to reveal Jehu's whereabouts, and thus by evasion and avoidance does not lie to the wri and thus not betray Jehu as well.

Opinion: Many of our fellow citizens do not look kindly upon Viola, and, as a consequence, they are ready to disbelieve whatever she says whether it be true or not; a baroque phrase, yes, but most people, whether they know it or not, are quite baroque themselves.

# 31

# Rebecca Escobar

A green-eyed brunette; the wri pegs her age at twenty-six-seven; she looks younger, much younger. Her relationship with her mother-in-law, the redoubtable doña Vidala Escobar née de la Viña Leguizamón-Leyva, is, at best, tenuous; in other words, they do not get along, well or otherwise. As Jehu once said about some other people: they just get.

The wri has learned from a highly-placed source in Jonesville, that the two woman do not 'enjoy each other's company.' The wri apologizes beforehand, here, but he refuses to surrender the name of the woman friend who supplied the information; the wri, too, can keep a secret, and that's the last word on that.

Rebecca, or Becky, as she prefers, is dressed in gleaming white: hat, gloves, and linen jacket and skirt. If not exactly a beauty a la San Esteban, she does present, as the Spanish say, other *encantos*; enchantments.

She is both relaxed and assured, and the wri, who is old enough to 1) know better, and 2) be her father, is equally relaxed and assured in her presence. The wri, after a rapid first impression, finds he likes the informant. He should be ashamed of himself for taking sides here, but he isn't, and he can't: la Caldwell-Escobar is a sunny type.

"I really don't know Jehu that *well*, you know. Ira and I first met him when we first came to work at First National, I mean, when Ira became associated with the Bank. First of . . .

"You must understand that Jehu was not Ira's supervisor or anything; I mean, he wasn't even a business major like Ira who attended A&M and finished up at St. Mary's. You know what I mean, don't you?

"Anyway, I saw Jehu at some of the Bank parties and picnics; stuff like that, but not much more. *And*, he is not at *all* interested in politics. Ira told me so. But I *like* him; I find him *nice*, and he's *friendly*, okay?

"I'm usually pretty busy on my Woman's Club work, and now, more recently, this winter in fact, with the Music Club, and what with taking the Cooke kids to dance music lessons, and what-all, I really don't have much time for . . . for other social occasions, don't you know. But we, Ira and I, did meet Jehu socially; early on, anyway; I think, or maybe I've heard, that he's engaged to Ollie Sans Teben; do you know her? She's a pharmacist here.

"And you *know* about what happened at Noddy's that night. As I remember it, it was just a little after eight o'clock, and we had just finished dessert after an early sit-down dinner when Jehu came in; he *saw* that we were through, and he had a surprised look on his face; not for long, of course, but you could *see* that he was surprised. I mean, it was strange, and I think Sammie Jo laughed; she'd been drinking some . . .

"But that was it; Jehu came into the dining room, and he was about to pull up a chair when . . . when Mr. Perkins, and no one had said a word up to then, anyway, Mr. Perkins said or asked, demanded, I guess, that, that, ah, that Jehu resign from the Bank; there and then. Ira and I were *so* embarrassed, you know, after all, we're *all* of us mexicanos, right?

"Jehu looked at Mr. Perkins and nodded, but not in agreement, it didn't seem like. He looked straight at Noddy; that's all he did, and then he . . . he just *walked* out. I don't think he said good night, or anything.

"Well, one hears so many things, right? Anyway, later on, on the way home, Ira said *he* thought it might have been a question of money. But that's all Ira said. He's very discreet, you know.

"And, *then*, another surprise! Jehu was back at the *Bank*! Just like that—hahahahaha—just like Jehu says, Just Like That. I mean, was it a joke on Noddy's part? Was he angry with Jehu because Jehu was late for dinner? The empty chair was there all along, you know. Ira called me first thing in the morning to tell me that Jehu was at the Bank. I was glad for Jehu; I mean, it was a bank holiday, but everyone was working inside. I mean, it was such a good job for him.

"Ira said that Jehu came in and went straight into Noddy's office just like any other Monday morning. About half-an-hour later, he was back at his own office and at work as usual. Ira says he, Jehu, worked through the noon hour, just like . . . like usual . . . and that *that* was it.

"The bank clerks couldn't have known, could they? And later,

Ibby Cooke, the V.P., well, he and Jehu had their Monday afternoon meeting just like always.

"I mean: nothing had *changed*. At *all*.

"At quitting time, Jehu, on his way out, stopped by Ira's desk and said, 'Well, Mr. Commissioner, did you enjoy your dinner Saturday night?'

"I think this is probably Jehu's and Noddy's idea of a big joke. I don't mind telling you that *that* Saturday night was ruined for Ira and me, I mean, for Ira and I.

"But I still *like* Jehu. I think he's nice and the few times I've talked with him, he's been very pleasant. Anyway, that's all I know except for the fact that he was also offered a job a couple of months later by the Barragán woman. Do you know *her*? *She* says she knows my mother.

"Do you think that there's a connection between the Saturday night thing and Jehu being offered a job by Viola Barragán?"

The above is verbatim and seriatim, and the wri accepts what he's been told. The wri listened very carefully to Mrs. Escobar and was saddened to think that this very young girl does not know, may not have an inkling, of what sadness, happiness, or sentiment are all about. Is it really possible that this is so? The wri sincerely hopes not, but he has no contradictory evidence, sad to say.

# 32

# Sammie Jo Perkins

Only issue of the Perkins-Cooke union; the wri sees a slender, brown-haired woman of thirty. Nothing personal, but most of those thirty have been lived on one of life's faster highways. She was divorced from Bradshaw, Theodore P. of the Dellis County Bradshaws at age twenty-three. Her present husband is Sidney Boynton; a so-called friend once said that SJ didn't have to change any initals in the bath towels, etc. Sammie Jo speaks Spanish very, very well, although this will not be evident here.

The wri would like to point out something that will be seen easily enough: speaking plainly is one of her trademarks. The wri points this for a purpose: he would not want for the reader to misjudge Sammie Jo's frankness for easy arrogance.

"Galindo, I don't *know* where he is, and I've known Jehu for a long time. He's a friend, and I don't judge friends.

"He doesn't care for Dad, you know, but he respects the way Dad runs the Bank. On the other hand, Jehu has no use for Ira, and that's no secret. But don't think that Jehu's afraid of losing his job at the Bank, 'cause Jehu could care less about that end of it.

"Tell you *what*, Galindo: I bet you he got to Becky Escobar. Wanna bet?

"Let me add this, too: if the Mexicans across town are worried that he *stole* money, shit on 'em. They're wrong as *hell*, and they're *full* of it.

"I'd say he was up at at Austin, wanting to go to grad school, but I don't know. I do know that's about all he ever wanted to do. Dad thinks he's there, and I bet Olivia knows where he is.

"Ollie wants things her way, and that's fine, but I bet Jehu wants her to have her way without *him*. Have you talked to her yet? If she had *any* sense, she'd either leave him be and forget all about him, or she'd *marry* him. Provided Jehu would have her. Ha!

"I *like* him, Galindo, though Jehu can be a real shit some times. Oh, I can, too, but we're good friends.

"Why don't you call Rafe? That is, call Rafe if you can ever get him to answer the phone; he's hell too, you know.

"But, that's it, Galindo, time's up. It's time for my dip; bye, now."

And with that, Arnold and Blanche Perkins' dau. smiled, offered her hand, and walked the wri to the door.

Sammie Jo is right: the Klail City mexicanos are a suspicious lot, perhaps more than they should be. It happens, however, as the wri knows, that some of these suspicions are well-founded on historical facts: 1836, 1846, and so on.

The reader cannot help but notice that Jehu is neither all saint nor all devil. Now then, that the truth unvarnished comes bubbling out of Sammie Jo's mouth is certainly worthy of note here.

# 33

# Arnold Perkins

The wri will borrow from Noddy Perkins's own description of himself: 'I'm a self-made man, Galindo. In some ways, ha-ha, that makes me a motherless bastard, right?'

In NP's case, the wri feels that there are enough biographical facts and data in Jehu's letters to Rafe Buenrostro. The wri, then, will not repeat what has been said. In his relationship with Belken County mexicanos, Noddy has his champions and his detractors. It's normal.

"Sure, Jehu and I have had our differences now and then, but that was to be expected; I'm not an easy man to get along with (grin with teeth showing). But it wasn't anything that couldn't be ironed out, it was business. Nothing more. You'd be surprised how well he took to banking. He has a healthy respect for money, that boy. And he's honest. Sharp, too.

"He's not much on social life, though. Oh, he dates the San Esteban girl . . . that's Emilio's girl, and I wouldn't be surprised if he also had something on the side. But, it's only natural, he's young. And, what the hell, we don't check up on our employees here. You know Klail City and the Valley, and it wouldn't take long for word like that to get around. I mean, it wouldn't take long if anything was wrong . . .

"Jehu speaks Spanish very well, you know; none of your Tex-Mex, either; I heard he'd been raised in part by a Mexican national, and that might account for it. And there ain't a thing wrong with his English, either; he's a Valley boy, and I guess the Army and the University helped there, too.

"He first started to work for us over at the Kay Cee Savings and Loan; he did mostly high risk insurance lending over there. I brought him over *here* after a year's experience, and he's a natural. I mean, he *likes* banking; he knows how to smoke out a deal and see it through; but, like I said, he's not interested in the civic stuff; don't misunderstand: he knows it's important for business, and he does it. As for politics, I don't even know if he votes or not.

"He's got a sense of humor, too. It's a bit pointed at times, but I can understand that; I was born poor myself. He worked well here, and no complaints. Of any kind.

"Jehu tolerates my brother-in-law, Ibby; Ibby's been at this bank some thirty years now, almost as long as I've been here, and that's before Blanche and I were married. Now, you'd think Ibby would have picked up what the hell banking was all about in that time: you take in money and you lend it out; you charge interest, and it's always the same money, and if you know what you're doing, you wind up with more. That's all.

"I can solemnly swear that Ibby still hasn't got *that* down.

"Now, when Ira came in last year, and that boy is full a-shit, he tried telling Jehu what banking was all about; Jehu just laughed at him, as he should've. Ira's pretty thick, and this takes me to something else: Jehu's not above getting into Ol' Becky's pants and pulling 'em down. I'm not saying he did, know what I mean? Besides, it's bad for business and makes for poor employee relations. Ha!

"I'll say it again: I'm not saying it happened. But, I know Jehu; hell, I was like that myself years ago. Ask old Viola Barragán! And, ask Gela Maldonado, too; ha! I bet Ol' Javier Legui *still* doesn't know about *that*. No matter, that was over thirty years ago.

"One last thing, Jehu's got a job here whenever he wants it. When he left here, he just said he *had* to go. There was never *any* question about money. In any way. I did hear something about returning to school, but like I said, if he wants his job back, it's his.

Confession: The wri took *and* smoked one of the proffered cigars and paid for it by taking to his bed for two days afterward. The wri should know better, of course.

The wri had no idea about those old Perkins-Barragán and Perkins-Maldonado liaisons. The wri can only say that all things are possible, e.g. the *affaire* Perkins-Téllez *is* a matter of record.

Question: Is there any reason for giving some, any, a little or no importance to these liaisons? Do Viola and Gela Maldonado recall them as vividly? Should they? And, at this juncture, does it matter? It may be better to consider that as water flushed and under the bridge.

Of more immediate concern, of course, is Perkins' careful assessment of Jehu. It certainly coincides with Sammie Jo's high opinion and reasons for his leaving.

In re the Becky Escobar episode, father and daughter may just be trading confidences here. And this is only in part, because Sammie Jo doesn't tell her father everything.

Does Macy tell Gimbel?

# 34

# E.B. Cooke

A widower for over a quarter of a century, this informant is the third of the six children of the Clayton and Myrna B. Cooke anschluss; of the six, four are still with us, three males and one female: the informant himself, Blanton, in his early fifties, Blanche (Noddy's wife), and Parnell, a forty-one year old congenital idiot.

The informant is a bit curt, peevish, snappish, even; but, the wri can attest that this attitude is not directed at his person, it is merely a trait of the informant. He was baptized Everett in the Good Shepherd Episcopal Church in KC; the B. stands for Blanchard, and thus he has a foot in both camps.

"Oh, I know you've talked to Noddy, and it doesn't matter, *in the least*. I also know what he thinks of me, and I don't care about *that*, either. I don't like banking, and I never have. I wanted to be a painter, Galindo, but the Bank and the Ranch, and our other investments and interests here and abroad could not be left to . . . Well, *someone* in the *family* had to be in it at this end, and Noddy is not *family*. Sammie Jo is, but he's not. Both Grover and Andrew died young; Parnell is not equipped for it, and that leaves Blanton and me. On the Blanchard side, there's not much to pick from, if you ask me.

"And I know about Jehu. I don't care to listen or to know whatever it was that Noddy said. Jehu's been here close to four years, and he and I get along; *he* knows I don't like the business, and so he does most of the ground work; I make policy.

"I really don't know if he *likes* the business. In point of fact, it's hard to tell *what* he likes or wants. I think he enjoys it, but I can't see him buried here for the next thirty years. He won't be wasting *his* life here. I know he's got some money saved, and how much, too; and, I don't find it such a shock that he left. I do know he wants to go back to Austin, to the University, and that's all there is to *that* piece of business.

"As you know, Noddy's my brother-in-law, and we don't get along. Never have. Blanche is a sick woman and has been for years; and Noddy's been no help *a-tall*. I don't care to get into that, but I don't want you to misread my feelings on the matter.

"Noddy is a ridiculous man; he doesn't know the first thing about ranching or about the oil industry, but to hear *him* tell it, well! But, he's strong, and he's devious, and that's his due, and I may be a damned fool for coming here every day for thirty years, but *someone's* got to keep a rein on him.

"Everything is *planned* with him. He even learned *Spanish* that way. Oh, I know what you think of *us*, but we're from here too, you know. And Jehu and Ira won't be the last Mexicans to work here, and I can promise you that much; but, if it were up to Noddy, ha!

"Jehu's bright, but he's also impatient at times. We work well together despite what Noddy says and tells everyone. I also know that Noddy says I don't know the *first* thing about banking, but he's wrong. I take no unnecessary actions, and I always make it a practice of letting Noddy have his way up to a point, and then, only in public. I don't *care* what other people think of me; I have my own life, I have my own friends, and Noddy's not a part of either one of them. Blanche is, but she's family and so is Junior Klail. And let's not get on the subject of that impossible sister of Noddy's, *please*.

"As for politics, that's what *we* are all about and *that*, Galindo, is merely farmed out to Noddy; look, we have businesses *everywhere* and Klail is but a part of it. The money started here years ago, and we started the town, from the Anglo Texan point of view, but Klail's only a part of it, and Noddy has a small part of *that*.

"I'm the cashier here, but I'm also the Secretary-Treasurer for the Corporation. Noddy knows perfectly well what *that* means. He tries to egg Jehu on, but that young man's too sharp for Noddy, and Noddy resents it. Oh, he resents it, all right. But, giving the devil his due, Noddy's been generous with Jehu's salary.

"As for me, well, I'm a painter, Galindo. A frustrated one and perhaps not a particularly talented one, either, but I can *read* people, I can read *character* . . .

"Now, would you care for a drink? We can have one of the girls bring us something."

Well! The wri has known Ibby Cooke for years (and years), about the time of the funeral for his uncle, the centenarian Judge Cooke (Walton H., Jr.), one of the founders of the Cooke-Blanchard clan. A funeral, by the way, which was excessively costly; tacky, almost. The wri, years later, learned that Noddy Perkins (married to Blanche Cooke less than a year) had been in charge of the funeral and floral arrangements.

Ibby's self-portrait does not jibe with the *role* assigned to him by Noddy; their mutual dislike may go even deeper than they realize, know, or imagine. Their opinions on Jehu differ, but only in a small degree. This may not be necessarily incompatible, it may be the same idea with two divergent points of view, that's all.

The wri must mark here that both men are steeped in the art of intrigue. They differ in method: Noddy uses spies, without their knowing they are being so used; he also uses certain base tactics: temptation (to Ira), false friendship and joviality (to the wri — Oh, yes), and a seemingly democratic chumminess (tout le monde). Cooke is more of an observer; he himself says he is, wanted to be, a painter; he is given, then, more to contemplation than to overt action. He doesn't seem to be intuitive (this may explain his failure as a painter) and by the same token, one sees him preferring pot shots to salvos. Instead of tactics, then, he prefers strategy, but this may be a semantic quibble.

The reader should consider, however, that the two in-laws have more in common than what may appear at first blush.

# 35

# Rufino Fischer Gutierrez

A descendant from the Cano clan. His paternal grandfather was the first Rufino Cano Guzmán, and his maternal grandmother, that grandame, was doña Florentina Anzaldúa Cano. Rufino is the son of the late Juan Eugenio Gutiérrez Guzmán; the Fischer part comes from don Fabián, father to Camila Fischer, who naturally enough, is RFG's mother.

A veteran of World War II as a member of the USMC, RFG was discharged in San Diego, California, returned to the Valley, passed through Klail City and Belken County and right on through Dellis County farmland; part of the 1749 Cano clan had lost some of the lands in the nineteenth century, and RFG has been buying some of them via the Texas Veterans Adms. program.

The wri has known for years that RFG and Bowly Ponder enlisted in the Marines together in 1943.

"Let's cut through here, Galindo; by the shade there. Let's see now, see that bent mesquite? The one next to that burned-up palm tree? Well, that mesquite was planted by one of the Peña boys that now lives in Barrones, Tamaulipas; no need to plant mesquites in the Valley, of course, but he went ahead and did it anyhow as called for in the grants; the mesquite's just about dab in the middle of the old Buenrostro land when the grants were first being parceled out. My cousin Israel Buenrostro has another bent mesquite on his land, and that one was planted by a Peña who lives on this side of the River. They're downriver people, as you know.

"The distance in American miles between the two mesquites is no less than forty miles, on a line. Our Fellow Texans own most of the land between the twin mesquites; that's a lot-a acreage, and I'm not saying I want it all, but I just happen to think that they've got more 'n enough, and besides that, we've already got the Leguizamóns around our necks, even here, in Dellis County.

"When we first learned that a Leguizamón from Belken was gunning for a Commissioner's post, we, the Dellis mexicanos, figured it was just one more nail in a lot-a people's coffins. And I don't think we were too far off, do you? As far as we're concerned, the water we got here in Dellis County runs, wets, and muddies up just like the one you-all've got over in Belken . . . know what I mean?

"I think that's as good a place to start as any: the land and the water.

"The last of the Ledesmas died last year; you knew Italo, didn't you? Well, ol' Jake Hendricks, the Dellis county clerk, told Arnold Perkins about it, I mean he told Perkins that the land was going to be up for sale; with this, then, Perkins had over a month's head start looking over the boundaries, the water rights, and what-all.

"By that time, the Landín family, the ones from this neck of the River, were up to their ears buying, selling, and trading off some land. One of the Landíns told us that Perkins wanted to sew up part of the Ledesma and Landín lands. That's fine with us, and business is *qeschafte* as my German grandpa used to say. But! what we didn't like or want or *need*, was for Perkins to share that land deal with the Leguizamóns. Those bastards are plain, bad neighbors; always have been.

"I'm going to tell you how we found out about *that* piece of business.

"The Landín family came to terms with Perkins but not for all the land; what happened was that we stepped in and bought some of that land ourselves, and then we turned around and sold some part of that to the Peñas from this side o' the River, and part to the Zúñigas; the Zees are related to the Peñas, and all three of our families are part of the Cano families from Soliseño; a family thing, then.

"Here, let me show you. (Pointing) There! no, over *there*, on the *other* side o' the River. See that settlement there? They're all Canos or Zúñigas there. But the telling of it here sounds easier than it was, though.

"Who *really* helped us was Jehu; he'd been invited to a political barbecue for that Ira Escobar guy, and Jehu decided to pay a call on Auntie Enriqueta Vidaurri before he went to the barbecue.* And it

*Mrs. Enriqueta Vidaurri died a month after Jehu left the Bank. She remembered him, as she should have, in her will.

just happened that I had decided to call on Auntie Enriqueta myself; she was ailing some, and she's family . . . Jehu and I met there, and he says for me to go to the barbecue with him, and that was it."

"They had one-a those MG's, and I said the hell with that, so we followed them out there. Jehu had Livvie San Esteban with him; my wife and I baptized that girl as her godparents, but you may know this, a-course. As for Jehu, my wife and I have known him since the day he was born in the Vidaurri lands in Relámpago. All this land you and I are standing on was nothing but cotton land some time back, and it was here that that protestant minister, the one Jehu worked for, was bitten by a rattler.

"Where was I? Oh, yeh; Jehu himself told us that that Escobar guy is a Leguizamón-Leyva, and it all became clear as glass, yessir. Arnold Perkins, the land deal, that young fool running for commissioner, everything. So, using that information, then, we got on our horses to work out our *own* deal.

"I hear tell that Jehu was let go by the Bank, runoff, kind-a. Is that true? If it is, then I bet the Leguizamóns had a hand in that. Although I must admit right off that I'm willing to believe almost anything that's said against those crooks.

"Jehu worked well with Perkins; he knows the land, how much it's worth, and he knows what's good for the Bank and what's not. Now, what he told me of the Escobar-Leguizamón-Leyva plans for that land may look bad to some folk, but Jehu is family, and he was giving us a fair shake, that's all.

"And, talking about Belken County . . . I'll tell you who showed up here: Bowly Ponder; yeah, he did. Got himself a county job, no less. Oh, yeah. Celebrating he was. He was in the Marines with me way back when, y'know. Since he wears a gun in Klail, and the county now, I guess, he can't drink there. What he does is to drive on over here to Dellis County, and he hells around some of the beer joints in Flads; those joints are right on the border levee. Probably goes across, too, knowing Bowly . . .

"I had seen him earlier, during primary time; he'd been drinking some, and he had one or two more for old times' sake. He likes his beer, old Bowly, and when he tightens up some, he loves to talk 'n brag.

"That night he told me how he'd given some Belken commissioner's wife a hard time; a *hurd* time, don't you know. Said he'd given her a ticket, that he issued an immediate summons, too, and then, for no reason at all, Bowly said it was all politics. I didn't say anything, and then he said that Arnold Perkins was hip-deep in something. That's nothing new, and I put it to Beer and Bowly, but later on, I came to find out that the woman Bowly pulled in was married to Ira Escobar's opponent in the primary. I'm not surprised; it's typical a-those people . . .

"But a fat lot a-good it did them. That guy is now a congress-man for our district, right? And the Leguizamóns can't see beyond their own damned noses, can they?

"Perkins jams a thumb full a-sugar in their mouth, and they don't even feel the dick when he sticks it to 'em. Serves 'em right.

"Well, Galindo, I'm worse than Bowly when it comes to run-ning off at the mouth, looks like. Hey!, I haven't even offered you a beer 'r anything. Come on!

"Tell you what, seeing as to how you don't make it to this part of the Valley much, you better plan to stay and have supper with us. Got me a white-tail last Spring (wink), damned thing ran right up my front fender and tied itself there. It's dressed, frozen, and waiting for us. Here, let me get the door."

RFG and the wri talked some more after the venison supper, but there was nothing new to report.

It certainly looks as if Jehu's information to RFG on the Escobar-Leguizamón tie-ins was no accident. And, of course, Jehu didn't do it for money, either.

One conclusion: Jehu is family conscious, and he did it as a family favor.

The wri holds no opinion on whether Jehu acted in good or in bad faith by divulging that piece of information to RFG, but there is the matter of business ethics here; Jehu, of course, does know Noddy far better than most and certainly far better than the wri.

The above is not meant to exculpate Jehu, however. .

# 36
# Bowly T.G. Ponder

In a three month period, our man's economic and professional lives have improved considerably. He resigned as a policeman of the Klail City P.D., and he is now a county deputy sheriff as well as a half-partner in two convenience-type stores.

He is now on his way to becoming a minor capitalist, and the wri has also learned that Bowly's two oldest sons are sure bets for graduation from Klail High School next year.

One further note: Dempsey Ponder, Bowly's youngest brother, is now the newest member of Klail's Finest.

"Well, all of this has been in the works for some time; George Markham recommended me to Scott Daniels himself, and he, Scott, talked to Big Foot, I mean to Wallace Parkinson, and Sheriff Parkinson saw fit to appoint me as a deputy here. I know Klail, I got my contacts here, and because-a that, I didn't have to move or anything."

The wri, an unreconstructed bully, dips into sarcasm this once to say that this is Noddy's way of keeping tabs on Bowly.

"Turned out right well, don't you think? And one thing about *this* job, I've got authority in the whole county, *and* a car. And expenses, too, Galindo. All in all, things are looking pretty good here. Listen to this: just last week, in this very car, I went and picked up Congressman Terry over to Noddy's airstrip. I did, and then gave him a ride home, too. No hard feelings, either; he knew I was just doing my job a while back when I stopped his wife. Show's you what he's made of, right?"

The wri, if he were Ponder, would take care when it comes to Morse Terry. The wri cannot believe that Terry is going to sit back and do nothing about the traffic incident.

Of course, if MT is a complete cynic, as Bowly certainly pictures him to be, then the wri invites the reader to join hands with him to pray for Bedelia Boyer.

"Dempsey moved right into the radio dispatcher's job, and this means that both Bobby Bleibst and Merle Gottschalk will be out on my old car beat. Ol' Dempsey's not cut out to be no riding-around man.

"And you say you saw Rufino Eff Gee over to Flads ta-other day? You know him, do you? Did you know that he and I go back a-whiles? Yeah, and I saw him myself not too long ago. I got me some old girl friends out to Dellis County.

"I understand from the Court House gang that Lieutenant Buenrostro's due out-a the Barrett's V.A. Hospital by mid-January. He sure did a good job on those murders, Galindo.

"There's the radio . . . gotta go; see you, Galindo."

From all indications, then, it does seem that Bowly Ponder is very much pleased with himself. This latest chat was not a total loss since it is now plainly evident that ex-Texas Ranger Choche Markham is still an active satellite in the Leguizamón-Perkins orbit.

The wri, without success, alas, has tried repeatedly to talk with Rep. Morse Terry: ten calls in four months (with the wri's name and teleph. no. each time) to no avail.

# 37

# Mrs. Ben (Edith) Timmens

Edith is married to Ben Timmens, one of the ten or fifteen attorneys employed by the Ranch, and thus the Bank. She speaks Spanish, Ben does not. (He hasn't *had* to.)

Timmens's wife, Klail City born, is the dau. of the late Osgood Bayliss, D.V.M. who was in long-time service to the Ranch. She is also the sister to Hapgood Bayliss who, until recently, served as congressman (D.-Tx.) for the Valley Congressional District.

"Pure fiction, Galindo: Hap isn't sick, he's tired. He's tired of Washington, of politics, and he's tired of being away from the Valley so much. Hap says that fourteen years up there is enough, and I agree with him. Ben and I put in eight years in the State Senate up at Austin plus another eight in Washington, and I know perfectly well how Hap feels. It's time somebody out of the family went up to Washington, anyway.

"Hap had told Noddy one whole year *before* the election that he wanted out, but Noddy kept putting him off. I honestly thought he *was* going to get sick. Anyway, I think Noddy shaved it a bit too close for *anybody's* comfort. A write-in campaign, really!

"Hap's marriage ended tragically, as you know, and being an old bachelor all these years, he plain wanted to come back home. The Valley's *home* and all our friends are *here*. And besides that, Washington's no place for a normal life.

"Well, it's been, what?, three-four months since the elections? Hap *looks* good and he *feels* good. He and Sidney are going down to La Pesca, Mexico for a bit of fishing; I think Sammie Jo'll join them in a couple of weeks.

"Have you ever been down there? Ben and I have, and we *really* enjoy ourselves. You know, you can't help but marvel how Mexicans from down there *differ* from Valley Mexicans. Well, not *you* exactly, but you know what I mean.

"You know, Becky and Ira both are still miffed at Jehu Malacara. Jehu didn't lift a finger; I mean, he didn't lift *one* finger during the entire election. Oh, he went to some of the barbecues, but it was like pulling teeth, and he never once spoke at a barbecue. Ira was hoping Noddy would've told Jehu, and that's what Ira says; so, Ira's still miffed, and can you blame him?

"Did Jehu ever tell you about something that happened at one of the parties at the Big House? It was a, a, a silly thing, really, but you know the Valley.

"I think it was Travis DeYoung's wife, no! it was Loretta; Wig Birnham's wife. Anyway, she either told a Mexican joke, you know, one of those Beto and Lupe jokes, or . . . no! it wasn't that either. Oh, I can't remember just now, but it was something anti-mexicano, don't you know.

"Really! I don't know *what* Loretta Birnham uses for eyes or for common sense. *We* didn't know what to say; I mean, Jehu was sitting right there 'n all. But she finally got up and drifted away. My God!

"Jehu didn't say a word. He just smiled a bit and then he nodded to himself, and then the next time he spoke, it was in the most broken English imaginable. He's a terrible tease, you know. Anyway, I didn't know *what* to say. I mean, I'm not prejudiced; I'm Klail born.

"Oh, wait a minute, now. He *hummed*; yes, I remember that. Know what it was? *Texas Our Texas*. I hadn't heard *that* in *years*.

"Speaking of Jehu, Noddy says that some of the mexicanos in town are saying that Jehu stole money from the Bank! That's *silly*. Where do you suppose they got *that* from?

"Noddy says he won't talk to them about that piece of business. I think Noddy's right. Javier Leguizamón told Noddy not to bother explaining things to *la raza* since he, Javier, would do it. And gladly."


This conversation, as many conversations, died a natural death. The wri, as old as he is, marvels still how public opinion with a phrase here and a phrase there turns and flips and flops back again.

It isn't because Edith Timmens recommended it, but the wri is now convinced that he can no longer put off his meeting with Javier Leguizamón. It is an imperative, at this stage.

In passing: Since Edith did mention what she is pleased to call the tragic end of his brother's marriage, the wri wished to clear this matter once and for all: Hap's wife (only dau of a former Texas Secretary of State) finally eloped with an opera singer; a tenor, as the wri recalls.

Since that happened so many years ago, 1) most people don't know this; 2) many more have chosen to forget it; and 3) the majority could care less.

The wri finds it interesting that Edith considers herself part of the KBC family, vide: the first paragraph. As interesting as it could turn out be, the wri has no time to discover what the family itself considers Edith.

# 38

# P. Galindo, the wri

Name: P. Galindo. Profession: writer, poet, journalist. Marital status: Married, widowed; married, widowed; married, divorced. Bachelor. Age: 52, and most of them spent with friends and relatives. Health: Precarious, even when he enjoyed the best of health.

The wri has spent the last two weeks in bed, or near it. His insides, or what's left of them, served notice that he needed a rest, some time-off. The running around after this act or that one is not conducive to rest, peace, and tranquility.

The ups and down, and the comings and goings, cannot but be detrimental to one's health, to one's peace of mind. Being back in the Valley has helped the wri recover some of his good spirits, if not his health.

The X-ray machine, unfortunately, doesn't lie. The wri himself saw the telltale pictures when he was going over his notes and first drafts. The wri, or so he thinks, is on the verge of arriving at the end of this work. It's merely a matter of a few more conversations.

As is usually the case, that which was thought to be a simple piece of research turns out not to be that at all. And, in spite of what has been said, by those who would know, and by the rest, those who know less but clamor the more, everything hinders and everything helps that which the wri would like to present and make known. A paradox, but here it is.

# 39

# Eugenio & Isidro Peralta: Klail City Twins

Eugenio is a debt collector for the Seamon Loan Co.'s Branch office in Klail City; he lives in his father's house. His father, Adrián, is called 'el coyote'. Not, by the way, a pleasant nickname to lug round. Eugenio and his wife, Hortensia (née Cáceres), have no children and they do quite well for themselves. Eugenio dabbles in politics through his father's good offices.

Isidro (aka Chirro) married Englentina Campos who died a very few years into the marriage; there was no issue. The subsequent nuptials (his father's phrase) were with María del Refugio Beristáin, who is very much alive. They have five (or six) children. (The wri did not, because he could not, give the exact no. of progeny in this case. There is, then, in this family, what is known as *un dudoso*, a doubtful one. At least this is what the wri hears bruited about). The couple, too, lives in the same block in which Isidro was born and on the same street as his brother and father. Isidro is an electrician (he owns his own shop) and you couldn't choke him for less than $15,000 in inventory, as we say in Belken.

The two were classmates of Jehu's and Rafe's, and, they, too, are Klail High graduates.

EUGENIO: "Well, if that's the case, then, I'll start first and then you, Chirro."

The wri, since he made no mention of it, wishes to add that the twins are frighteningly identical. The wri looks upon them as decals of each other; a singular similarity in gestures, facial expressions, and in an antisocial habit of scratching: backside, crotch, sideburns, etc.

EUGENIO: "Jehu? Why I knew him before he was born, as we say. When the Korean War came up, he was among the first to be called up by the Reserve. I, by the way, have never been in the Army; failed the physical, you know. Maybe it's because I'm a *ciclán*; yes, that may be it.* (Turning to his brother) You failed yours, too, remember? You had TB as a child."

ISIDRO: "That wasn't the reason."

EUGENIO: "What? Everytime we talk about this, you go and change . . . "

The wri stepped in before the Brothers Peralta started to raise their voices right in the middle of Klail's mexicano downtown section.

EUGENIO: "*Okay*. I also work for the Bank, on a contract basis; they hire me to collect their bad debts. I collect for Seamon, a-course, but I farm out to the Bank, as needed, see? I don't get much from 'em, but money fits all pockets, is what I say.

"Jehu told me about the job; he explained it, too. If I collect, fine, if I don't, that's okay, too. They, the Bank, make a write-off; a bad loan, see? Now, if I do collect from a skip or somebody like that, I get a cut, and then the Bank comes out ahead, too; they get their money back and the interest or part of the collateral, right?

"Jehu also pointed out that Goyo Chapa, some time back, used to do this, but then he tried to get cute on 'em; yes, he did. Goyo reported that he couldn't collect on some of the bad debts, damfool, and then it turns out that he *had*; some of the people came to the Bank to see about their accounts 'n all, and there it was, all laid out, in black and white. Goyo'd tried to get to 'em, see? Damfool thing to do, I say.

"So what happened? Not much: Pen State, all the way! I think he was stored up for a couple-a years or something like that.

"Me, I got the job on Jehu's say-so. But, I'll tell you this, we never got along well in school; this was years ago, a-course.

"Jehu also helped me secure a loan to fix Pa's house a bit; told me *what* kind-a loan, what *terms*, too, and business like that, you know. He knows his stuff, all right.

---

*Ciclán:* A Spanish peninsular term for any male animal born but with one testicle. (From the *Dictionary of the Royal Academy*.)

"As Jehu says: 'The Bank can't lose; don't you trust us, now; we're in the business of making money.' I like the advice, all right, but the way I see it, that's no way to protect your job, giving away secrets like that. And now, I hear he's leaving or that he's left, one of the two."

ISIDRO: "Yah; and the other mexicano there'll freeze you in your tracks. Yes, he will. He doesn't even want mexicanos coming *in* the Bank."

EUGENIO: "Yeah, you're talking about Escobar; that's his name. *I* don't know him; someone said he was from Jonesville; but, nah, I don't know him at all."

ISIDRO: "Well, I don't *either*, but he's still a pain."

The wri would like to explain that the twins are speaking to each other; it's as if the wri weren't there at all; that is, they speak *with* but not *to* him. They look like two veteran actors who've been on the road so long, they know each other's lines and everybody else's, too. The wri decided not to intervene.

ISIDRO: "What *I* am-about-to-say-to-you, stays here; either that or nothing doing."

EUGENIO: "You got my word on that."

Isidro looked at the wri, who had no choice but to nod his assent: discretion, discretion. The wri begs forgiveness or yet another interruption, but he is a bit uncomfortable with this pair of o' jacks. The Peraltas look like two drops of water. It's amazing. (Isidro is somewhat elliptical in his descriptions; it may have to do with his profession. Who knows.)

ISIDRO: "A long time ago, a November I think it was, Sammie Jo was here in Klail on a school holiday, and ol' Jehu, on furlough then, stuffed her like a turkey. That was years ago, okay? But another time, farther back, in high school. A summer, okay? So it wasn't the first time, you got that?"

EUGENIO: "Can you beat that, Galindo? And now, some ten years later, they're at it again."

ISIDRO: "Yah, and in the Big House, too. He's crazy."

EUGENIO: "Got-to-be, but opportunity's like getting bald, it comes by the one time. Hold it, Chirro: I said *b-a-l-d*, don't you . . ."

The wri, word of honor, attests what is here recorded was what was said, nothing less, nothing more.

EUGENIO: "Go on."

ISIDRO: "I'm an electrician, as you know."

Eugenio nods in agreement, and they both look at the wri who also nods. The wri, no fool, knows he is not of the company.

ISIDRO: "All *right*, in a subcontract I got from Tommie Kyle, a small wiring job for Ranch security, I got to see Jehu with her again; Noddy's girl. In bed."

EUGENIO: "There are five of us who know now."

THE WRI: (The wri!) "Five?"

ISIDRO: "Yah."

EUGENIO: "That's right: you, us, and them."

ISIDRO: "My turn . . . "

The wri wanted to scream as loud and as long as his failing lungs would let him, but he didn't. And then, he lusted after a drink *and* a cigarette; luckily for him, he forewent all three. The wri was both wise and fortunate in this regard.

The wri, by the way, is grateful he has no twin to dog his steps. When the Peraltas invited him to supper, the wri excused himself; he apologized, profusely, but nevertheless, he excused himself.

To avoid any, *any*, possibility of a misunderstanding, the wri affirms that he gets along well with the twins, on a one-on-one basis. The wri, on occasion, has enjoyed a mano-a-mano with one or the other, but it happens that the wri (honesty above all) finds it disquieting, unnerving almost, in dealing with xerox copies in human forms.

A weakness, true, but there it is.

# 40

# Lucas Barron

Dirty Barrón has owned-run-managed, whatever, some ten or so beer joints-parlors-places, whatever, in the thirty-years the wri has known him. Dirty is much older than the wri, and is, then, a member of the wri's preceding generation: the old Revolutionaries. (Guzmán, Leal, Garrido et alii). Dirty knows the wri well; he also knows Jehu and Rafe, and with little exaggeration, half of Klail City. Mexicano Klail, that is.

He speaks English well enough, and as most Klail City mexicanos, he has and claims relatives on both sides of the northern and southern banks of the Rio Grande. Ruddy-faced and blue-eyed, Dirty has a high-pitched (almost hysterical) voice not uncommon to the Valley.

"So it's come to this, has it, Skinny? Man can't even serve a friend a free bottle-o beer. Humph! How about a Nehi orange, then? Some iced tea? Good enough; tea it is. I'll tell Crossy to bring it to us; here, we'll sit at my table.

"Cross!, go across the street there and tell Noriega I want a pitcher-a tea.

"So this has got to do with Jehu, does it? Well, what can I say? I know him, and I like him. And I think highly of him, too. Now, you're not going to hear no bad mouthing from me, no sir. Knowing you, a-course, I know you want the truth, and the truth's what you're going to get, okay?

"Well, I hear a lot in here, but talking's cheaper 'n knowing, as they say. Ah, here comes the tea. Two iced glasses, Crossy.

"Okay, now. Talk here, in my place, is that he was fired, kicked out, and then landed on his ass out in the street somewhere. That he was light-fingered, too, but that's bullshit. That this and that and t-other. Now, as far as I know, no one from *this* side-o town has talked to one Anglo Texan; not one. Or with any A.T. who knows anything, at any rate.

"Now, your old friend Polín Tapia blew in here and was talking up a storm, but how reliable is your old friend, I ask you? Right? And I'll tell you who else talks and talks, but talk is all he does 'cause he ain't allowed to talk at home, and that's Emilio the Gimp. That's right.

"Don Manuel Guzmán says little, you know *him*, and they should listen to what he says. Don Manuel says that if the Anglos had a case or a charge, they'd-a gotten Jehu and right quick, too. Yessir. Our fellow Texans ain't about to close their eyes to somebody making off with their money. And . . . it ain't a race thing, either. It's a money matter with them. Don Manuel says there's nothing to it, kid probably got tired, that's all. A-course, you won't hear shit about Jehu 'n all when don Manuel Gee comes in here.

"And what can you tell me about Andrés Champion? Anybody says anything—anything—about Jehu, and Andrés'd just as soon break that expensive cue stick a-his over your head and then poke you in the eye with it. Yeah. And he ain't the only one, 'cause Jehu's got friends of all ages. You know that.

"Some other folks talk about women trouble, and that's a mite ticklish, I say. Jehu's had his share, maybe more, but the old men, the *viejitos*, they're not about to step in on *that* piece o' business.

"When it comes to the young guys, they're saying that Jehu got to one-a the girls there and you know how *that* goes. But, that too is talk, and nobody really knows anything. And they, and you, and I know *why*: Jehu's no blabber.

"And that's it, a lot-a talk, and a lotta shit, too, but nothing else. No, sir.

"And how 'bout you, Galindo? What do you hear?"

Lucas Barrón is a first-class barkeep and almost as old a listener as the wri. (He interrupts less, too). Dirty does all right for himself: he owes no money and even less favors, as he says. The *Aquí me quedo* Bar belongs to him lock, stock, and barrels-o'-beer; and, if anyone he doesn't like begins to raise any kind of hell, he'll tell him where the door is. He'll tell him the once, by the way, and no more. The second time, the bouncer, Cross-eyed Moreno, takes over from there.

Dirty didn't say so, but he won't put up with Jehu being bad-mouthed, either.

Confession: The wri wonders now and then if he has as wide a circle of friends, firm friends, as Jehu enjoys. One can't have too many good ones; no question.

The wri plans to seek out Polín Tapia for a second go-round.

# 41
# Polin Tapia

Vide Pt. 24.

"Nothing, Galindo; I'm telling you straight; I don't know a thing, really. It isn't that I'm avoiding you. I just don't know.

"One *hears* things, but that's not *knowing*, is it?

"Oh, and don't think I've been digging here and there, either. No, sir. I have my own affairs to run, after all. I, ah, I'll be working part-time in Morse Terry's local office while he's up in Washington, don't you know. And, as for the rest of my time, I, ah, don't know; I mean, it's nothing definite, the Ranch or the Bank, MAYBE, but, ah, I, ah, I don't know in what capacity. And if not *at* the Ranch, then maybe at the Cooke Lumber Yard and Paint; you yourself know that *I* know about paint and such.

"And to change the subject on you: Ira is doing very, *very* well, and he'll take very good care of Klail City's interests on the county level, yes, he will, you bet. You just wait and see. Ira's got talent, yes, he does, and he knows the full meaning and definition of the word *gratitude*.

"Ira told me, just the other day, that Jehu's old job's been passed on to a relative of Morse Terry's, and I'll tell you *why*: Ira's many obligations on the County Commissioner's Court impede his progress at the Bank. Impede, Galindo. At this time. But look to this: Noddy knows and recognizes the work Ira does there, and he's not blind to Ira's talents. No, sir."

The wri does not interrupt PT: no need to. Sooner than later, PT, who knows nothing, as he says, will open up like a Rio Grande floodgate. A matter of time, that's all. The wri confesses to a certain advantage in all of this: he knows PT better than PT knows himself.

"At the Ranch, and I know little or next to nothing, everything's in order. They've all returned sunned and tanned and healthy from their trip to La Pesca, Tamaulipas. As for Sammie Jo, she decided not to go at the last minute; I think she flew up to Houston or Austin some place to see some relatives or maybe they came down to the Valley, one of the two. You know, of *course* you do, and don't shake your head, dammit, you know they own those two planes and that little jet, so those people come and go as they please and *when* they please.

"I'll tell you who was under the weather, though. Mr. E.B. Cooke; he's okay now, thanks to God. Attorney Bayliss looks fit, and he's recovered from that serious illness a-his which came over him sudden-like during the elections, remember?

"And I can't complain; I'll be at the Congressman's office here in Klail, like I said. It's Noddy's doings a-course; it's his way of showing gratitude, although I really didn't do very much, if you know what I mean."

The wri shakes his head, raises an eyebrow once in a while, crosses and uncrosses his arms, but does not interrupt the flow.

"And, there won't be a divorce, and *that's* final. Sammie Jo says that Sidney needs her, and that she'll stand by him. How about *that?* Kid's got spunk, right? She's a Perkins, yessir! No doubt-a 'bout it.

"And, and, and there's no one, anywhere, who can deny that both Noddy and the Ranch didn't do right by Jehu, 'cause they did. But what can you expect? Written in the stars, it was. If you can't show gratitude, you can't show gratitude; it's like a lack a-class, is what it is. Well . . . I better not go into that; not now, anyway."

The wri's ears perked up some, and they stayed that way until:

"But according to Ira all's well at the Bank, and one would think that Jehu'd never worked there a-tall, ha!

"And you, Galindo? How's the world treating *you?* You still look a mite piqued."

The wri is grateful (one must always show gratitude) to his friend's kind solicitation in re his health. And the wri *is* grateful, because while PT has

'a weakness or two
and rarities, too'

one does not fling and forget a thirty-year friendship, after all. Polín Tapia has damn few friends who'll listen to him for very long. The wri (a weakness and a rarity) is a first-class listener. In this case, better than that. In this case, it is of the utmost that he listen carefully and well.

A word of caution: PT isn't that damn privy to the Ranch doings. He reads the *Klail City Enterprise-News* (owned by-the-reader-knows-who) and PT, as most, reads it cover to cover every Wed. and Sun. That's all.

# 42
# Vicente de la Cerda

Owns a Dodge truck blessed and later baptized as "Hang in There, Klail City." VdlC knows Jehu well, since Jehu was a child, he says. He approaches the wri, and he'd like to get something off his chest. He says:

"Yeah. See this truck here? Jehu loaned me the money for it. Well, no, lemme back up a bit and start off again: he fa-ci-li-ta-ted the money. He didn't sign no note, a-course, but he helped. Israel Buenrostro, and he's a good one, too, he signed the note.

"Jehu's good people, and he'll drink a beer now and again.

"Truth to tell, I don't know much about that old Leguizamón-Buenrostro feud, but I heard, and not too long ago neither, that Jehu put the old block and tackle to Becky Escobar, get me? He jacked her up, Galindo, on blocks. And you know she's married to Irineo Escobar, the one who calls himself Ah-ra. On blocks, Skinny, and that's why he had to leave the Bank.

"But what the hell! He's young, ain't he? And he ain't no capon, right?

"Well now, the one I *don't* know about is the pharmacist; don't know her either, other than she's a San Esteban. Owns that little green car, and those guys over to the Blue Bar say, but it's all talk, 'kay?, they say that if Jehu was serious, *if*, 'kay?, if he was serious, then it'd be with her. She's a piece — hold it, Mr. Galindo — I say she's a piece of class, she's educated. Just like Jehu, see? Been up to Austin, both a-them, right?

"Over to the *Aquí me quedo*, some-a the guys there say he got to Sammie Job (sic). She's Norberto Perkins' pride and joy, she is. They had a, a, a arrangement, right? That's the word, right?

"It's possible, Mr. Galindo. Now some-a the guys there say that this has been going on since high school, can you imagine that? Probably nothing to it, but that's what them guys over to Dirty's 'r saying. The worst they'll say is that Norberto Perkins didn't care. That's bullshit, Mr. Galindo, that's just being mean, isn't it?

"I've also heard that Rafe Buenrostro and Sammie Job sometimes back it was, were pretty close. Ol' Cross-eyed Moreno, yeah, Crossy, he said so. But where he got *that* is a mystery. My guess is that Crossy knows nothing about nothing. Ha! With that right eye looking straight at his nose, what can he see, right? Cheap-ass talk, if you ask me.

"Rafe Buenrostro knows how to take care a-himself. He's . . . a,a,a,a . . .

The wri does not believe he should put words in anyone's mouth; the wri *supposed* that the word looked for was *discreet*.

a, a, let's see, I got it: he's quiet, he can keep a secret. Yeah, that's it.

"And that's about it, Mr. Galindo. If I learn anything else, or hear anything else, or something, I'll remember . . . "

The wri wishes to go on record that he gives credit, but of that, little, to the talk at the *Aquí me quedo* Bar and the Blue Bar. But, he also recognizes that truth comes in different packages and at different weights. Thing to do, then, is to listen, to hear, to assess, and to see what truths drip out from time to time.

Vicente de la Cerda, older than Jehu and thus nearer to the wri's age, is hardly an unbiased source, obviously. Still, he volunteered, and the wri does not turn such informants away at the door.

# 43
# Emilio Tamez

About Jehu's and Rafe's age; once a frequent barroom brawler, a marriage at age twenty-five put a halt to that way and style of life. (It isn't germane to the matter at hand, but ET's wife is one of the shortest, teensiest, women the wri has ever seen anywhere. She's shorter than short.)

Tamez still makes the rounds although not as much nor as frequent; the regulars at the Blue Bar say that the day or night that Emilio gets into another punch-up, that'll be a general announcement to the world that Esthercita Monroy, the hand that rocks the cradle, has now kicked the bucket. Emilio, instead of fighting, has now retired to safer ground: talk and little else.

He drives a pickup, as he has for some seven or eight years, sun up to sun down, picking up and driving here and there, the numerous Blanchard heirs. And they *are* numerous.

Emilio is known as The Gimp; this came about as a result of slipping on some broccoli (while running atop a refrigerator car) and breaking his knee and assorted bones. This kept him out of the Army; had this not happened, the Army would've still not got its mitts on him: Young Murillo, an otherwise peaceful youngster, once took a knife, under provocation, and sliced one of Emilio's ears off; Murillo caught it in mid-air, and handed it to Emilio, who threw up.

Many cheap shots were then hurled at Emilio after this incident.

"My brother Joaquín says that the Ranch has some seven 'r eight railroad cars on the First Street siding and all loaded up with barbed wire; it's replacement wire, and it'll be up by the end o' May. New posts, too, and all cedar. Ha! Joaquín signs for *everything* that comes there for the Ranch.

"It's a pleasure to work with that kind of people; the Blanch-

116

ards may not have *all* the money in this world, but I bet they beat their relatives the Cookes, yessir.

"And look at this, now: they treat me with courtesy. Consideration, even. It's a damned shame to have to say it, and I mean what with friends here and all, Galindo, but at times, the Texas Anglos show more class than the Texas Mexicans and I'm no Anglo lover, right? But, I know what's right, and I know how to be grateful, and I'll work like a dog. And, and, and what about some of us who have a college education 'n then piss-off the job; can't hold on to it. Talking about Jehu, and a friend-a yours, I know, and no, he ain't here to protect himself, but it don't matter a bit; I'd say the same thing if he'd walk through that door, there.

"The Anglos'll put it to you, but we give 'em cause, too, you know."

Emilio Tamez talks, as the saw says, to hear himself talk. The wri finds it ridiculous that Tamez knows, or would know, what opinion, if any, the Blanchards have of the Cooke cousins, and vice versa. To add to this, he shouldn't forget that the alphabet around here begins and ends with K for Klail. As a mathematician woman-friend of the wri is fond of saying: 'One should be able to distinguish between what is important and what is essential, in all things.'

"Okay, then, and what about them garage sales a-theirs? Hey? Well? They're held at the Ranch, and they're held for *us*, the workers. That's first class clothing we're talking about here, clothing that's barely been used. And cheap to buy? Lemme tell you, Galindo. Yeah, and the money? Know what they do with *that*? Why, they give it to their *church*, that's what!

"They don't *need* the money; they give it to *charity*. Yeah, they do.

"All right, let's see, now, and just how long did Jehu spend with his holy rollers? And selling bibles, from what I hear . . . Shoot, and now look how he wound up. Making us *all* look bad. Yessir.

"We Tamezes are hard workers, yes we are. And we don't take lip, neither. And Jehu? Well? Well? When has he *ever* faced anybody down in this cantina? In *any* cantina? College ruined that guy; got himself educated, and then he couldn't measure up in the street or in the Bank!"

It's entirely possible that Tamez had had more than his usual limit. The conversation/monologue jumped from here to there back again; no one at the tiller, as we say in the Valley.

The Tamez have always been hard workers, no doubt on that at all. And, favorable comment in this regard has been made elsewhere, but hard work shouldn't be worn as a special medal; other Valley mexicanos work just as hard. And as long, too.

The wri knows that Emilio says what he says relying on Common Law: What's said in a cantina stays there. If one's been drinking, more's the reason.

The law has to operate this way; life would be intolerable, otherwise.

# 44
# Arturo Leyva

A degreed accountant; he has been married these twenty years
to Yolanda (only dau. of doña Candelaria Murguía de Salazar alias
'The Turk' and her late husband, don Epigmenio, aka The Knight of
the Woeful Hernia). Leyva is a year, perhaps two, younger than the
wri; he has known Jehu for years.

"They, whoever *they* are, well, they had better not come here
with stories, trumped or not, about Jehu. Not to this place, and not
to this person. Ah, and if they do, they had damn well better be pre-
pared to face Arturo Leyva head on. Right now, tomorrow morning, any day of the week, Sundays included."

The wri interrupts to say that this informant speaks of himself
in the third person. Always.

"Arturo Leyva does not permit cutting remarks of any kind
from anyone about himself or about his friends. If Emilio Tamez or
anybody else, talks that way, away from the cantina, at the ball
park or wherever, then that somebody is hereby put on call. Arturo
Leyva will take matters in his own hands; Arturo Leyva says he
won't stop with Tamez; it matters little or not at all whoever that
whoever is or may be. Anybody deaf around here?"

The wri should like to point out that AL is not the biggest man
in Klail City; he's tough enough, though, and better than that: he's a
man of his word; what we call *un macho cumplidor*. He has, as
such, a sense of friendship, loyalty, and he knows what they stand
for.

It must also be said that Jehu, in his teens, saved AL's bacon in
an *affaire de coeur*; an *affaire* that had it seen the light of day,
would have been fatal for AL. The wri uses his words carefully; if

Leyva's mother-in-law, The Turk, had learned, smelled out, that Arturo did, in fact, betray Yolandita, the Valley would have had one accountant less on its census rolls.

"That boy is and has been a bulwark. He'd been at the bank *one year*, and at the end of that one year, three mexicanas got jobs there; yes, they did. And he did it 'cause he hired 'em; they needed to be there, he said. And he didn't put the make on 'em, either. No sir.

"That's the way it is. Now, that he likes his fun is something else, but let he who is *without* cast the first one, right? Damn right. Hell, he's a Valley boy; he knows what to do.
"Remember Old Echevarría, whom God now graces, remember what he said about Jehu? 'Leave that boy be! What can any of you teach him that he hasn't already seen or lived? Being an orphan's a bitch, and it gives but one lesson: if you quit, you die! Leave him be, I say.' Yeah, Arturo Leyva is here to remind you all, if it bears repeating, what the Old Man said. And he said it in this cantina. 'Leave him be.'"

The wri is pleased to say that Arturo invited him to a beer; with AL, this is a sign of trust and friendship. The wri was unable to accept, sad to say. The wri is not getting any better.

# 45

# Esther Lucille Bewley

Some four years younger than Jehu (she says so), she has worked at the Bank since graduation from KCHS. Unmarried as yet, a bit on the short side, but pretty enough, her hair is short, curly, and blond. Blue-eyed, she is a bit too thin according to the wri's own preferences. Of pleasant voice, Esther learned her Spanish out in the small ranches, fields, and cotton rows which dot the Valley and which surround Klail City, and everything else.

"Uncle Bowly said you had come round and talked to him a while back. You didn't know he was my Mom's older brother, did you? Well, he is, and that makes *me* a Ponder on my mother's side.

"Let's see, Jehu was a senior in high school when I was only a freshman, and I really had a crush going, let me tell you. But, that was years ago. He never knew it and didn't till I told him here at the Bank some three years ago. And when I did, he just smiled.

"Now, there *is* something I need to tell you, Mr. Galindo. It's something I know."

The voice dropped with finality but with assurance and force. When she said she knew *something*, and despite her young age, she seemed a sad old woman sentenced by some higher authority to reveal certain secrets no one else in the world is privy to.

"I do, Mr. Galindo; I really do. You see, I've *watched* Jehu. Closely. And I can add; I can put *two* and *two* together as well as anyone. But I, I, I'd *never* do anything or *say* anything to hurt him.

"He's a good person, Mr. Galindo.

"Not *once*, Mr. Galindo, did he ever order me around. He just asked me if I knew my job, I said I did, and he said, 'Good enough.' And then (smile) he said, 'Watch your ass, Esther; there's a lot of bastards in this world.' He's a gentleman, Mr. Galindo.

"But that *other* one! Mr. Texas A & M over there. Why, I speak better Spanish than him; and know what else? He wouldn't lift a finger to help anyone. He once told me to get him some coffee, and I told him, quiet like, but I told him to go get it hisself, *himself*. And there's a word in Spanish for guys like him, right?"

At this point, Esther turned reddish and her old age, laying in wait, passed over as a breeze by a baby's crib: light, airy, warm, calm.

"But I know something, Mr. Galindo, and I know about the fights, too. At the Big House, and at the office. And you know *what?* Mr. Perkins was righter than he *knew* and Jehu *still* beat him, Jehu beat him at his *own mean game*. Oh, I could've kissed him, Mr. Galindo.

"After the shouting in Mr. P.'s office, Jehu walked out-a there, winked at me, and then gave me that smile-a his; he then turned to Ira and pointed at him, you know, like with a toy pistol? Well, he did, and he smiled again. But it wasn't the smile he gave *me*. Know what else he did then? He called me over, and he was standing not two feet from Mr. Big-Shot's desk, he called me over 'n said, real-serious like, but smiling the while: 'Esther Lucille, the world's full of sons-of-bitches, but killing's against the law, so you've got to skin 'em once in a while, just to let them know you're here.' That's exactly what he said; word for word. And then he said, 'Want to flip to see who makes the coffee?'

"See what I mean?"

The wri, who is not half the cynic he thinks he is, noticed how Esther Lucille's too-blue eyes danced and almost clouded over. No, she didn't cry, but had it come to that, the wri, yes, the wri would have dissembled and understood. (Costs little, worth a lot.)

"It's not important that I tell *how* I know, but I do. And, I know about *both* of them, Mr. Galindo. *Both* of them. You see, Uncle Bowly knows, too, but he'd never tell Mr. Perkins. Never. He told Ma, though, and Ma told him not to say it again. To anyone. Uncle Bowly's foolish, but he's not *silly*; the cops, well, they *know* a *lot*. And, they *hear* a lot, too.

"Besides, and you don't know this; no, you don't. Jehu's cousin, the cop?, the detective?, well, he got Uncle Bowly out-a some scrap in Flads, in Dellis County. Yeah, he did. Rafe fixed it up, Mr. Galindo; whatever it was. So, you see, Uncle Bowley'd never say a word; I wouldn't either, and I won't, but, but Jehu . . ."

At this point, Esther motioned with her chin: first at Noddy's office and then at Ira Escobar's desk. Esther looked thinner still and sadder, too, but thinnish and all, Esther Lucille smiled that smile which will accompany her, taw by aggie, to her old age.

The wri, before old age comes and erodes Esther's youth, wants for Esther to be happy, and, if possible, happier for a longer time than she's ever been.

It's not too much to ask.

# 46

# Don Javier Leguizamón

Our man has arrived at seventy-plus arduous years of fleecing his fellow man (and woman). He's religious, he's a patriot, and an inveterate user of the first person singular.

The man, at various times, has been a merchant, a rancher, a dealer in wholesale contraband (north to south, south to north), and a faithful follower of his instincts. He was born, as the saying goes, with both eyes open. He expects to leave this vale in the same manner.

More, much more in fact, could be said about the large, vast, Leguizamón family, but the wri recognizes that one needs German patience and scholarship to cover all the Leguizamóns of the world in depth.

"Not meaning to brag, and I say this in all possible modesty since at my age now and, yes, even as a young man, have I ever sought to stoop so low as to bring attention to myself. I, then, as I was saying, I, in great part, am responsible for Jehu's position at the Bank. Accordingly, then, I, am responsible for whatever happened, señor Galindo.

"Sad to say, but I did recommend Jehu to Noddy, and there he went. A couple of years later, when another post opened up, I made sure that that one went to my niece Vidala's boy, Ira.

"I knew that Jehu was in dire, pressing, ah, need of a job and hence my recommendation to Noddy. I know Jehu, and have known him since he was a child. In point of absolute fact, he worked for me in one of our stores here in Klail."

The wri has lost count of everyone who has known Jehu since his childhood.

"I can't deny, hide the fact, that I'm somewhat disappointed that Jehu did not help us during the elections. As it turned out, he wasn't needed, but no rancor, señor Galindo, none at all. And, if the opportunity again presents itself, I'd recommend him again. Would do so, yes, and highly and gladly, too. I'm here to tell you I would; one either stands by one's word or one fails, and I, we, the Leguizamóns, are not built that way. Firm is what we are. "You well know that . . .

ACHTUNG. The wri knows nothing of the kind.

. . . all of our male lineage, of those of us born in the past century, I happen to be the lone survivor. Our family, thanks and glory be to God, is flourishing, and I no longer have to see or oversee the day-to-day business affairs. No; I now leave *that* to them, to the youngsters.

"I, always, and first and foremost, have dedicated myself to family first and to business interests later. If one takes care of the first, why, the rest comes tailing right behind; an easy conscience, taking care of bringing no injury to one's neighbor, and if one finds an opportunity to do someone a favor, one does it and gladly. And I don't ask who the recipient is, no sir. All *I* want to know is: how can I help, when can I help, and *where* can I help. And that's it, señor Galindo; and it's said in all modesty, and if I have pride, then it's my humility that I take pride in.

"I know I have my detractors, but I'm above that. Truly. At my age, I see no reason, none, why I should worry, unnecessarily, over what is said or thought about me, as erroneous as that thinking may be.

"One isn't perfect, and I'm the first to admit it, by God. But, one's lack of perfection should not cause one to lose control or to follow the devil's ways and byways.

"Work, family, order, and progress, seriousness of purpose, sobriety, and charity to the unfortunate is the Leguizamón way of life. Not our very own personal motto, no, but we do try to follow those precepts. Assiduously.

"That favor to Jehu was not the first extended to that young man, and I stand here before you to say that it won't be the last. And, although he is a relative of the family that thinks ill of us, that may even work to destroy our good name and reputation, we, the Leguizamóns, know about favors, about extending a hand, and I am not the kind that expects payment or recognition. At any time."

Goodness! But be *that* as it may, the wri prefers that the words spoken by JL remain as a personal monument: inviolable and intact.

The wri maintains that he will not descend to the plains of irony.

# 47

# Jovita de Anda Tamez

Married to Joaquín, the eldest of the Tamez brothers, Jovita was a bit wildish in her teens. This has passed, and the informant has given several children, and according to some, very few restless moments to her husband. Others say otherwise.*

"It's been years since I've seen Jehu Malacara. Years. And, I haven't seen Rafe for longer than that. Now, I used to see Rafe when he'd cut through here on his way to work at Lucas Barrón's place; it was one of those summer jobs, and Joaquín and I would see him go by as we sat on this porch here.

"As for Jehu, señor Galindo, as I said, it's been years. And it isn't that Klail's that big a place, but what with housework and the kids and what-not . . . You know.

"My brother-in-law, Emilio, comes by once in a while, and usually just about every Sunday for the barbecue when he and Esther come calling.** We talk about everything under the sun, a-course, but it wasn't until recently that I heard what had happened to Jehu at the Bank last year. But this is old news.

---

*The wri, and he doesn't quite know how to broach this, heard stories-rumors-base gossip, whatever, many years ago, that (sometime after the Korean War) Jovita accommodated (if that's the word), that she accommodated Jehu; others say it was Rafe. Mention is made of this (unfounded as it may be) because the rumors were not cantina-based; a woman friend of the wri, and he has a few, also mentioned it in passing years ago.

**This Esther, of course, is Esther Monroy, Emilio's wife, and not Esther Lucille Bewley, Bowly's niece. Probably no need to so identify for the careful reader, but the wri is compulsive when it comes to accuracy.

"Anyway, what I hear *now*, is that the pharmacist San Esteban is selling her end of the business to her brother. That she plans to *live* with Jehu; up in Houston, I hear. I heard that from Emilio, and I can't recall where else, but as far as hearing it, I did, and more'n that, too, I also hear that the pharmacist is using part of her money to pay whatever money it is that Jehu owes the bank. Emilio himself told me this.

"Can all this be true? You see, señor Galindo, I also heard that she wasn't going to help him; that Jehu has a new job in Austin, and that he sends part of his salary to the bank; a special arrangement between them, is what I hear.

"I told this to Emilio, but he says it isn't so; he also says that the pharmacist is a fool who goes around throwing her money away.

"I don't know *what* to think; I *know* Jehu, and I can't believe what people say about him. Oh! I just remembered something else I heard at Efraín Barrera's store. I heard that the Leguizamón family is helping Jehu. Joaquín says I'm a fool if I believe any part of that.

"But truth to tell, I really don't know much, and I'm telling you what I hear, and that's it. But . . . you hear it so much, see?"

The wri notes that Jovita (six kids older) is still a handsome woman; this is merely an observation on part of the wri.

The reader is free, as always, to accept or to reject whatever Emilio Tamez says.

In re Olivia San Esteban's plans, the wri, for now, does not plan to speak to OSE, or to her brother, Martin.

# Part III

# A Penultimate Note

The reportage mode ends with Jovita de Anda Tamez.

The wri has additional material, but it's his opinion and personal guarantee that none of it would amplify the case at hand.

That material, therefore, is considered unnecessary since writing isn't merely a case of filling in page after page of what could prove to be repetitive information.

An end has to be reached somewhere, and this is it.

# Brass Tacks Are Best; They Last Longer

Despite the unalterable fact that certain people, more or less responsible people, or others who should know, and those who do know better, and despite the many friends and backers of Jehu Malacara, and he has those who do protest friendship, (most of the Klail City mexicanos) they say that Jehu is guilty.

They are not, however, precise as to what the crime may be; this is the least of their worries, they say. The wri has been witness to the tone, to the manner, and to the *how* they say it, and he thinks that if some of your basic igneous rocks were handy in Klail City, that Jehu, were he to return, would need to grow some extra eyes to dodge them all.

The wri also heard that Jehu had been dishonorably discharged from the U.S. Army, and that he was fired twice from his post at the high school. Some also said that he loafed on the job at the Bank; that he was there as a showcase. Other notes attest that because of his shady dealings, unspecified, other aspiring mexicanos will not be able to work at the Klail First in the future.

Tucker French, the local V.A. adviser, says that Jehu attended The University of Texas on the G.I. Bill, and Lauro Parás, a former assistant principal at the high school, says that Jehu left twice for better paying jobs; Mr. Parás also says that Jehu was a better-than-average teacher.

The wri offers Perkins' own testimony as to Jehu's work habits and abilities.

None of the above has dented public opinion in any way. A matter of Caesar's wife, it seems.

Other voices say that Jehu hasn't married (he's now thirty-years old) because of his fear of women. The running around is just a cover-up, they say.

Others say that his bachelorhood is owed to *other* preferences. The wri can only shake his head. The public is used to having its way when it comes to interesting stories that do not coincide with evident truth. Nothing new, then.

The pillars of the local churches (The Apostolic and the several

Protestant branches) decry his lack of formality (sic) and seriousness. His lack of faith, too, and hint darkly at his probity at the Bank.

The wri thinks that Jehu has faith although, perhaps, not too much in his fellow Klail Citians.

The *mater familias* say that they knew all about him; they merely waited cross-armed, patiently, and with saintly resignation, one supposes. They knew, they say, that Jehu would come to a bad end. Would get his, others said.

The *pater familias*, *hombres machos*, nod in agreement and all agree with their consorts. The p.f. say that the majority is always right. (Originality, in Klail City, is a sin).

The wri rests in the knowledge that someone who calls himself a friend will see to it that Jehu learns of his new reputation in Klail City. There are people in the world who love to pass on bad news in the guise of friendship.

The wri, getting down to those well-known brass tacks, is convinced that JM will return to KC someday; he is, after all, a native son.

When that day comes, he should take great care. It may be that every mutt and cur on the mexicano side of Klail City will line up to pee on him.

*O tempora o mores.*